The Hourglass That Swallows You

Timeshome
Book 1

Alexander Albret

Originally published in Great Britain by Timeshome Media Ltd

Copyright © 2024 by Alexander Goren Albret.

All rights reserved.

The right of Alexander Albret to be identified as the author of this work has been asserted in accordance with sections 77 and 78 of the Copyright Designs and Patents Act 1988.

All characters in this publication are fictitious and any resemblance to real persons, living or dead is purely coincidental.

No part of this book may be reproduced in any form or by any electronic or mechanical means, including information storage and retrieval systems, without written permission from the author, except for the use of brief quotations in a book review.

ISBN: 978-1-0687335-0-5 (Paperback Edition)

ISBN: 978-1-0687335-1-2 (Ebook Edition)

www.timeshomemedia.com

For Mum,
I wish you could have read this final version.

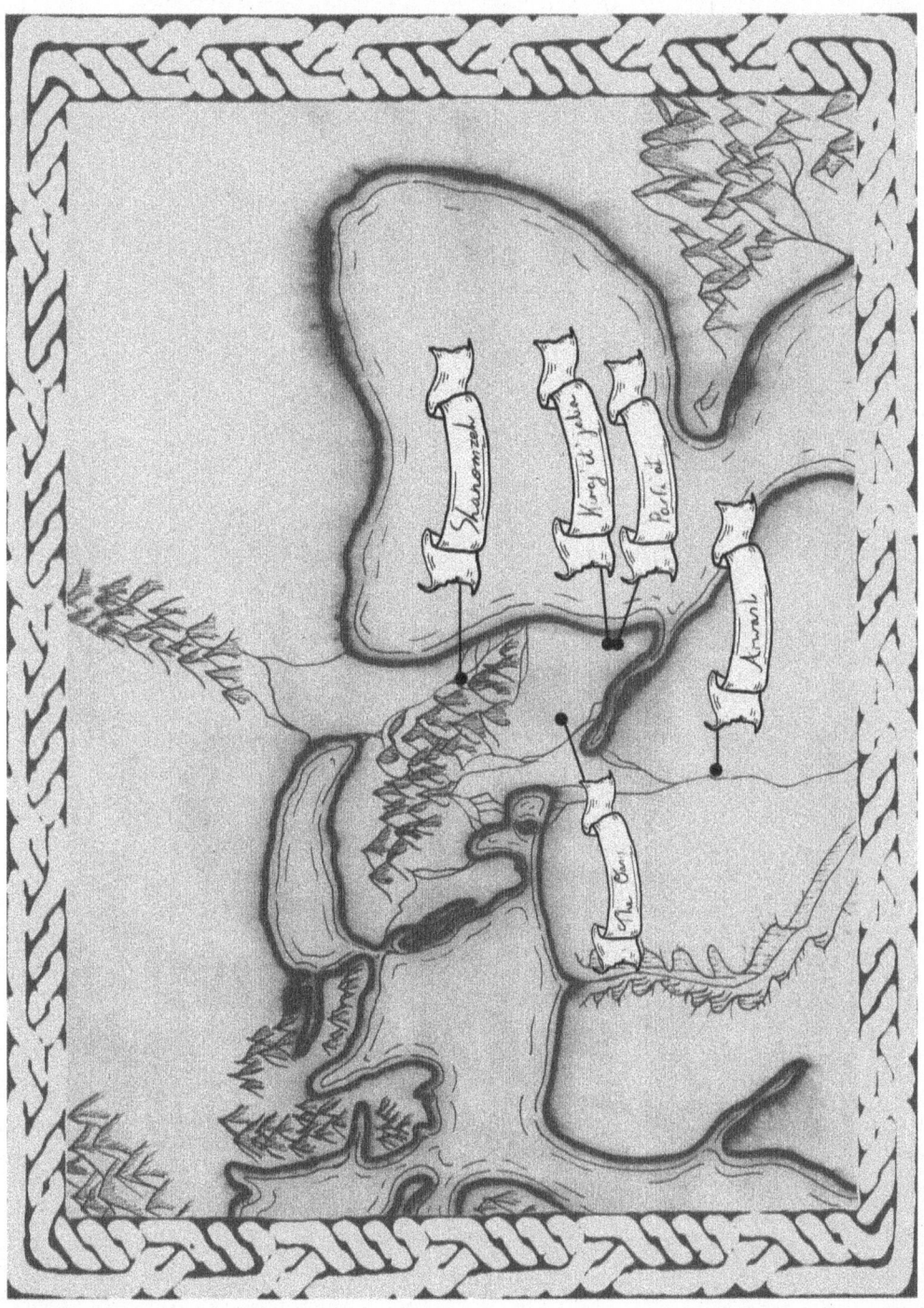

MALD

IN THE PIN-PRICKED fabric of the midnight sky shines a brilliant blue and green pearl. 'Ifa Shadelna, the sister planet, continues its waltz with the silver moon.

Below, watching that galactic waltz from in front of a large desert tent, is an Ozymandian figure dwarfed by the midnight sky and vast desert. His loose desert shawl imprints the outline of a wraith against the sky.

At his feet a small fire has been allowed to almost entirely burn out. The little light the embers cast reflect a dull liquid orange onto his face and arms, but not much else.

From the East blows a cold, desert-night wind. The hair on his tanned skin stands on edge. He tightens his shawl around him, which causes his curved cavalry sabre and silver Faijh a'ilatr[1] to shift on his person uncomfortably. He readjusts them. Then he unconsciously rubs his hands together, as if trying to clean them. Something, he can't quite put his finger on it, but something has

---

1. Faijh a'ilatr [fai.jh.a.il.at.r]: side small sword, or dagger held on the side - lit. "Faijh" side, "a'" lesser, "ilatr" sword

risen him from his bed, and forced him away from his wife and his family before dawn.

From the depths of the tent a fluttery low-pitched female voice whispers out.

"a'Mald, my shivauz[2], where have you gone?"

Mald responds back gently.

"I'll be back inside in a moment my shivai. Go back to sleep."

The sounds of rummaging drift out from inside the tent. His family are shifting around. He can just make out his son's voice briefly but can't make out the words.

Then the noisy silence of a dark night falls over them.

Mald lets out a sigh and adopts a soldier's stance without thinking. His hand rests lightly on his curved sabre. He looks out over his desert. Then, at a thought, he looks back to his caravan train and his own small desert camp.

The small fire by his feet is set apart from the larger fire still going by the camp. There are less than half-a-dozen tents set up around the central fire, forming a defensive ring.

One of his silver-white horses, off some distance to the camp, lets out a snort which mixes in with the dull snoring and low bass of his two dozen tribesmen and tribeswomen's voices.

Three of them are still awake, idly chatting by the larger fire and passing around a ceramic jug. The others were resting.

A wave of tiredness comes over him. Once, a long time ago, he could stave off his tiredness through sheer force of will.

Now... the sand is ever shifting, and the worlds will continue their dance.

He rubs his hands again.

But that unease won't dissipate.

He mentally counts out his current guardsmen:

---

2. Shivauz (m) / Shivai (f) [shi.vauz / shi.vai] : A term of endearment used by lovers – lit. "Sh'v'" the concept of light, "Shiva" meaning star, "-auz" (male) or "-ai" (female) 'one who does', so Star Maker or Light Maker

The Hourglass That Swallows You

One to the east, leaning on his camel. He was young, lean, and tall. He was definitely one of Mikautr's boys.

One to the north, propped up on his long spear. Mald couldn't remember his name, but Ilatr was sold on him. That was enough.

One to the south. The Eastern-Eye style mace, that made him infamous, clinks awkwardly against his sabre as he raises a ceramic jug to his mouth, and takes a long swig.

Damn it Ilatr.

If anyone else had been drinking like that there would be a reprimand later but as it stood, he trusted his second-in-command with his life.

Finally, one to the west-

-A sharp spike of fear causes Mald to tense up.

There should be another.

Where was the Big Man?

As if responding to Mald's fear a large figure comes out of one of the tents. Mald relaxes, but his heartbeat doesn't slow. Mald's jaw clenches. If he didn't have a good reason for it the Big Man would face a tongue-lashing tomorrow.

The Big Man turns and kneels by the central campfire to warm himself. With a laugh one of the other tribespeople around the campfire pass him a jug.

Mald's jaw unclenches as he breathes out slowly. All seemed right.

Out of the dark a thought strikes him. Was it a sound? Or just his imagination?

He casts his gaze over to where his horses are resting out west. From here he can only see a few of the dozen of them. And he can't see any sign of the boy.

Mald marches off towards the horses at a quick pace and with an angry click.

"If that boy is asleep-" he mutters to himself as he marches. "The 'Shadel[3] have him. And if he let any of those horses wander off-."

Behind him a heavy crash of ceramic explodes the night silence.

Mald spins towards it and back to the camp. His eyes reflect the orange glow as they adjust to the sudden change in light. It takes him a moment to figure out what the sound was.

Before he can figure it out comes a sound like someone ringing a bell, metal on wood.

A high pitched yell pierces the midnight air.

Mald's body moves before his mind takes over.

His eyes scan the campsite as he runs.

Hunched over the Big Man towards the fire are three shadows, dressed in dark clothing. With a grunt of effort and a push of his sword he forces them all back at once. He doesn't engage aggressively, but instead adopts a defensive stance, beckoning them to come attack him.

Mald notices why he was being so defensive, as behind the Big Man, Mald can just make out three of his tribesmen scrambling backwards on the ground. The Big Man was holding off the shadows as if he were a bear protecting his cubs.

Mald's adrenaline kicks in and his legs beat harder upon the sand. His sword sounds like a hissing cat as he draws it.

"'Ifacho! To me!" Mald's voice echoes on the dunes. In the tents the sounds of tribesmen and tribeswomen respond, still dazed by sleep, to the call of their leader.

More dark figures appear from the east emerging as if from the sand itself. Mald steers himself towards them.

Another ringing sound echoes off of the dunes.

Mald looks over towards the ringing.

Ilatr swings his mace with all his might against the shield of an attacker. The mace shatters the shield with a massive bone-shattering ring. The man holding the shield is knocked backwards. He

---

3. 'Shadel ['.sha.del] : Spirit, soul - lit. "'sha" fox, "del" eye, or fox eye

crumples screaming on the ground, his arm and shield in pieces. Ilatr closes the gap between him and the raving man on the ground. He raises his mace.

"Ilatr, to the dawn! To the East!" comes Mald's command.

Ilatr instinctively pauses, mace in the air. He catches Mald's eye and nods. Then he turns back to the man on the ground and swings down. The attacker screams holding out his shattered arm. Ilatr stops the mace abruptly and grunts towards the man with a sadistic grin. The attacker winces, fearing further pain. Ilatr instead spins on his feet, leaving the man writhing on the ground, and sprints off to help the small group of tribesmen holding off the attackers around the fire.

Mald reaches the man on the ground and slows down to take a breath. Exhaling he takes stock of the situation and scans the area.

There don't *seem* to be many attackers. And this isn't enough for a full scale attack, nor even for a proper raid. Not to mention that this was *our* territory... Who would be so brave as to do something like this?

Mald looks down at the attacker Ilatr had been fighting. The attacker was squirming backwards, hate and rage in his eyes. The attacker draws his Faijh a'ilatr and throws it weakly at Mald with his offhand.

It doesn't come anywhere close. Mald, with his sabre still in hand, swiftly dispatches the man with a clean precise swipe across the man's neck. The attacker falls backwards clutching his throat spluttering until his last breath. Mald wipes his blade on the dying man's dark clothes.

Suddenly a young boy's high pitched yell carries on the wind.

Mald's eyes open wide, his calm assessment of the situation stolen away by fear. His first instinct is to look towards his horses, but, no. It didn't come from where the horses were.

His tent.

The thought hit him hard. He swings towards his tent. With all the strength and speed he can muster he sprints towards it, passing by most of the fighting.

His heart skips a beat as he sees a dark figure emerging at a run from his tent.

A cry erupts from the depths of Mald's chest as he brings his sword up to swing at the dark figure.

Time stands still as Mald swings.

The swing is too high.

Without warning the dark figure collapses forward and Mald's blade misses.

Panic strikes Mald.

He swings around to see a simple dagger, with a dull jade oval encrusted into the hilt, skewered deep into the man's back.

Mald's head turns from the dagger to the inside of the tent.

Understanding dawns on him.

He lets out the breath that he hadn't realised had built up in his chest.

In front of him, looking defiant, is the woman who had just thrown the dagger. Standing at the threshold of his tent, the dim light of the burnt down embers reflect a face very similar to his own, but sharper and more feminine. Each breath is heavy but shallow. Her eyes scan every shadow.

Mald looks from her and peers around the tent, and then into it. The bodies of two dark-figured attackers lay sprawled out on the floor within. Mald turns to her with a quiet desperation in his eyes.

"a'Jali[4], where is my Talia?" He says before adding with an edge of fear to his voice, "Is she safe?"

His sister, the defiant woman, signals by nodding behind her. Huddled in front of her children with a dagger in hand, like a crouching lioness, is Talia.

Hand over his heart he nods at Jalila.

---

4. A'Jali : A' + name usually denotes familiarity and affection between two people - lit. "A'" little, lesser, or small

Mald gently pushes past his sister to hug his wife and his children. Jalila shrugs off the silent thank you as she moves aside.

"We protect each other. As we always have little brother," she says quietly as she moves out of the tent. Outside she kneels down to pull out her dagger.

Mald lets out a heavy sigh as hugs his wife. "I- You-" he slows his breathing to try and find the right words. "-I should have been here."

They let go of the embrace.

Talia swallows. "Go to the girls..." is all she manages to say through the shock.

He nods and looks over his shoulder towards a dark corner. Huddling in the corner of the room behind one of the hanging ornate rugs are his two daughters. He stands and moves over to hug them both at the same time.

The little one, Kita, is the spitting image of Talia, with jet black hair and large brown eyes. She hugs him back with all of her might. Diwa, his teenage daughter, also hugs him as hard as she can. She has more of her father in her, and the family resemblance to Mald and Jalila is strong.

The shock of the situation still hasn't left her. Mald kisses both of their heads in turn.

"I'm here girls. I'm here," he says.

He pulls away softly. Then turns to Talia. And then around the room.

"a'Jheal?" he says looking around.

A young boy appears from behind a mat on the other side of the tent, breathing quickly and shallowly. He is trying to stop himself from shaking. In his hand is a small sapphire-encrusted carving dagger. The ground below looks black and oily in the little light of the tent. The blade weeps a tear of blood from its edge.

Mald puts the puzzle together quickly.

"Come to me, a'Jhea. Come my boy. It's alright," Mald says.

Jheal scans the tent first and then focuses down towards one of the dark-clothed bodies. His body shudders violently at the sight. He quickly looks back up at his father.

"They came at us from nowhere. I couldn't think-" his voice is shaky. Mald gets up and quickly hugs the young boy.

"I-I did as you said. Dad. I-".

"You did very well my son. You did as I taught you and you did what you had to. Be proud."

Mald gently takes the knife away from his son as he pulls away and takes a stand.

Jalila with a flick of the tent flap stalks back into the tent. She has her dagger in one hand and one of the assailant's swords in the other.

"Where is a'Sha?" She says simply, her level tone belying the fear in her eyes.

Realisation hits Mald.

He jumps to his feet, then turns to Talia with a sharp edge in his voice.

"a'Tali stay here and protect the girls."

She nods and beckons the girls over to her.

Mald returns to his son and gets on one knee to look at Jheal at the boy's own eye level.

"Protect your sisters. Protect your a'ijd[5]."

Jheal nods, his body is shaking but his eyes are determined. Mald cups his son's face to bring the boy back to the present. Jheal nods again, more sure of himself this time.

Quickly getting to his feet Mald signals for Jalila to follow. With a short sharp fwip of her dagger the assailant's blood is gone.

They leave the tent at a run.

"He was on lookout with the horses," he says between breaths.

"You gave him look out duty alone?" Jalila says, "he is as young as a'Jheal!"

---

5. a'ijd [ah.'.ea.d] : lit. Mother

"He requested it-" Mald says, "he said he was old enough to do it by himself!"

A sharp, horrible horse's whinny cuts him off. Mald knew a horse's death cry when he heard one, and this was one of his mares.

Ahead a thin plume of smoke is rising from a low fire near the horses and where that horrible cry originated.

Jalila begins to sprint.

Mald sprints to catch up to her pace.

Then Jalila stops abruptly at the crest of a dune.

"a'Sha!" She cries before her figure drops down behind the dune.

Mald's breath catches in his throat as he reaches the crest.

Blood and smoke reflect the dying light of the little fire a'Sha had made. It takes Mald a moment before he can compose himself.

The corpses of horses litter the sand and dirt. A dozen of his pride silver-white horses have been slaughtered, with their necks roughly cut.

His eyes search desperately between them for any sign of the child, or any remaining attackers.

Mald can't speak as he looks around the killing ground.

"a'Sha!" Jalila's shout echoes as she runs towards one of the downed horses.

Mald follows her more cautiously.

Underneath the mare a small way, knocked unconscious and dyed red with horse blood, is a child the same age as Jheal.

Sha.

It takes Jalila a moment to reach him. As she does she immediately begins to frantically pull him out. The horse is heavy, but it only covers his feet.

A moment of strain and the boy is out.

Freed she leans over him muttering his name over and over again.

"Please. Please, a'Sha be okay-"

a'Sha doesn't respond.

Jalila doesn't notice Mald kneel beside her. She leans down closer to the boy.

"a'Sha," she pleads, "a'Sha please be okay."

Suddenly a'Sha opens his eyes with a whimper.

He clutches his shoulder in pain.

a'Sha begins to blabber, words and sentences not fully forming.

"a'Ijd, I couldn't do anything. She was so hurt. I couldn't-"

"What happened here boy?" demands Mald.

His tone seems to cut through the shock. Jalila jumps at her brother's tone.

a'Sha continues clutching at his shoulder in pain, but sees his uncle and mother clearly.

"I ran Uncle," he says. "I heard the screams- I was lying down with my fu'ait[6]- and- and then the horses began screaming, and there was so much blood, and- and- I had too. I couldn't-".

He begins to babble again without forming proper words. Tears pour out of his eyes. His mother hugs him close. He breaks down and starts to sob harder into his mother's arms.

"Enough a'Mald," snaps Jalila, "you're scaring him."

Mald stops and turns her an angry eye.

"Enough," she repeats softer. "He needs to rest."

Mald sighs and nods at her. Then turns back to a'Sha.

He takes a deep breath before speaking.

"You did well to hide," he says softly as he gets down to his knees to look at the child in the eyes at his own level.

a'Sha initially doesn't meet Mald's eyes.

"You did well Sha," he repeats as he puts a hand on the boy's shoulder and uses his other to gently force the boy to look at him.

"I am not angry with you. Fear and pain can cause you to lose focus. Anger, from within or outside, can make you focus."

a'Sha nods.

Mald nods and releases the boy. Then he looks around. Years ago

---

6. Fu'ait [fu.'.ait] - Horse

this would have been enough to ruin him and his tribe. Even now the death of a dozen of his silver-white horses was enough to force him back into banditry. Or at least it would have been had he not become Tijjikauz's guardian of this ocean of sand.

Still it hurt his heart, and purse, standing as he was staring at the horses still-warm blood streaming on the desert dirt.

A glisten from the mare that was on top of a'Sha catches his eye.

Staring closer he notices a'Sha's knife embedded in the horse's neck. A precision stab, through an artery, not a rough cut.

With an unreadable expression he turns back to a'Sha.

"Both of you get back to Mother and stay safe," he says softly, "who knows if any more fools are out there."

Jalila nods and gets to her feet. Then she lifts up a'Sha and walks off in the direction of their tent.

Mald is left alone with his thoughts. He rubs his hands as he looks around.

How did the boy's faijh end up in her neck-

The sound of boots on sand drags his attention. From the direction of the camp comes the man with the mace, Ilatr.

"We are safe, akal'Mald[7]. There doesn't seem to be any more of them," he says.

Mald lets out a sigh.

"They killed our horse-" Ilatr continues, his jaw clenching as he speaks. "Those -..."

Without realising it his fists also clench and unclench by his side as he follows his own train of thought.

"When we find out which tribe did this, the shadel will have them. This is our land, akal'Mald. Ours."

Ilatr's voice trails off.

Mald looks from his second-in-command and then back to his horses. He rises slowly and moves with purpose over to get a closer look at a'Sha's fu'ait.

---

7. akal'MALD : akal' + name denotes respect, gendered male

He kneels. Then puts a hand on the grey horse with a'Sha's knife embedded in it and pulls the dagger out. He cleans it on the dead horse's mane and neatly places the blade into his belt.

Slowly he rises back up to his feet, and looks around searching for something, anything. Any clue as to the attacker's identity.

"The south? The western 'Ifacho? Someone new? Who dares raid so close to our territory…" Ilatr's voice drifts back to him. "A decade we have been guardians here. We are known. These men were either brave or forced."

Ilatr has one hand on his sabre, the other has a firm grasp on his mace, and every word he utters is making him angrier and angrier. Despite that, through his anger, he notices Mald looking intently at something.

Partially covered tracks lead away from the camp. Ilatr's eyes narrow.

They are too long and too… rectangular. Horse and man and… a cart of some sort.

"Get someone to follow these tracks," says Mald staring.

Ilatr nods, and breaths out slowly to quell his anger.

"Yes akal'." He says keeping his tone level.

Mald continues, "I have a feeling… that this wasn't just a raid."

Mald stands and looks down at Sha's knife in his hand.

"I don't think they were aiming to kill us."

Ilatr spits on the ground at the mention of the raider.

"Goat piss Mald. Those dogs killed the Mikautr boy. He hadn't seen enough dawns by far. They were here to kill us and steal Diwa's dowry."

Mald looks back towards his own tent. Using some sand off of the ground he cleans the horse blood off of his hands.

"We lost more of our family here tonight.-"

Mald sighs.

"-But death claims those with a name as easily as those without. If they were here to kill us- all of us- they would have been better off picking us off around the edges of the night, not try to kill our horse. Yet it feels like they got what they came for. We had more horses than those that are lying dead on the ground, yet they are gone. Taken. Whoever did this... They wanted our horses. And they will pay dearly for it."

SHA

SITTING low out over the desert, the sun is slowly rising; the wandering planet is coming to meet it. The black-to-blue-to-golden dawn light mixes in the sky.

In the lee of a rock sits Sha watching the travelling Home of the Spirits meet the sun. A brief dry heat blows in from the west and out over the desert.

Sha glances westward to embrace the wind, and to stop the wind from causing his black hair to cover his eyes.

He was supposed to be watching his family's remaining prize-horses and camels, to make sure that they don't graze too far from the camp, but Sha's eyes are instead lit up watching the sky.

As he does so his mind bounces from story to story of the Shadel who live there. This is the first time in his life that he has seen this sight, and he can't take his eyes off of the Wandering Planet.

A whinny breaks him out of his daydreaming.

His mind bounces uncomfortably from story to memory.

His breathing quickens and his heart threatens to burst as his eyes scan for any sense or sign of the attackers.

He takes a moment to calm his rapid breathing, as he was taught by his Uncle. Slow in through the nose, and deeply out through the mouth. His eyes search the horizon at a frantic pace.

Without warning the wind catches his scarf and it flicks into his face.

He scrambles to drag it down in fright. The smell of the horse's blood on the scarf wrinkles his nose.

Then as if drawn to them, his eyes find the freshly dug horse graves, signified by a mound of rocks, to the west.

And that was it. There was nothing out here but sand and wind.

The ever-altering sands of the 'Ifacho are calm.

He closes his eyes and heaves a sigh.

But flashes of blood and his fu'ait's laboured last breaths keep invading behind his closed eyes.

He looks back around to the remaining horses to distract himself and breathes out another sigh.

It has been almost a day since the attack but his muscles still tense reflexively at every small sound.

To distract himself he idly begins to pick up and test out some stones, throwing the ones that don't meet his standard. Picking out a small sharp stone, he looks at it. It's about right. But not perfect.

He reaches for the dagger on his belt, only to find empty space.

He lets out a sharp click. The stone will just have to do as it is.

Another whinny makes him wince.

He ignores it as best he can and gets to work on the wall of the overcrop he is under.

A high-pitched cry steals Sha's attention from his work. He looks up sharply from his writing.

An almost unnoticeable beige flash scatters by the edge of his family's camels and horses, but Sha's quick eyes catch it.

Only a small desert fox.

Sha quickly refocuses on his task on the wall; noticeably not watching his horses or camels.

A low rumbling sound begins to build in intensity.

Hooves running.

Horses sometimes run. Sha doesn't take notice.

Thwack.

A stone cast from a horse's gallop hits the wall next to him.

He looks up in time to see some of his horses running, ears down in fear. Sha's eyes go wide.

He drops the stone and jumps to his feet, a wild yell forming from his throat. In front of him the horses are galloping around erratically.

Before his body can move a silver-grey horse stops in front of him with a spray of dust and sand.

Sha looks up wild-eyed and sees Uncle Mald in the flowing, deep bright-blue desert wear of their people on the mare's back.

"Did last night teach you nothing, boy!?" yells Mald. "The sands are always shifting, you must notice it."

Mald swings his horse around to look at the galloping horses.

Sha can't bring himself to look at Mald. Instead he focuses on the fleeing horses.

"I was paying attention-" he says.

Uncle Mald's silence is his only response.

Sha stops himself. Excuses don't get him anywhere with his Uncle.

"I'm sorry- I don't know what happened akal'Mald."

"You weren't paying attention," Uncle Mald is still looking out towards the horses. He shakes his head.

His gaze turns and lingers on the writing on the rock.

Finally his gaze settles back on Sha.

"I expect all of my horses to be rounded back up before we leave... or else Shiva will have you."

Sha's eyes flicker in panic, yet he finds disappointment, not anger, in his Uncle's eyes.

The observation instinctively turns Sha's panic to anger.

"I am ready for this, Uncle. I am."

"Then do what I say. Go. Now."

The Hourglass That Swallows You

Sha has his feet planted in the sand in defiance. It takes him a moment to understand through his anger.

He lets out an angry huff and then runs as fast as his legs can take him to the nearest horse, a mare that hadn't run too far, and jumps on her back.

She wasn't his fu'ait, but she would have to do.

He sets off with speed to round up the other horses.

MALD

MALD TAKES a deep breath as a'Sha gallops off to try to round up the horses. He watches briefly then shakes his head. Dismounting his mare he walks over to what a'Sha was carving into the rock.

He runs his fingertips over the top, feeling out the straight-lined and angled writing.

The symbols are arcane to him, writing from the west.

Thinking of the people whose language this was makes him reflexively show disgust.

"That was uncalled for," a woman with a soft voice comments from behind Mald.

He doesn't turn around.

"a'Jali, you of all people know he needs to learn to keep his focus... the winds blow, the sand shifts and the hourglass turns."

Getting to his feet, Mald continues.

"And, more importantly, he needs to learn to do what his leader says, when he says it. It will cost lives if he doesn't."

Mald sighs, looking to his feet.

"If we don't break him and teach him to learn, the desert will. I saw the anger in his eyes. That boy is far too strong willed."

Mald turns to his sister and smiles a toothy grin.

"A lot like we were."

She doesn't wear a pleasant look.

He laughs.

"And our father would have done far worse than I just did."

Jalila shakes her head.

"Our father was not a great man to emulate" she chides as she moves over to the writing on the wall.

Mald takes a half-step back to get out of her way as she pushes past. "Ah come on a'Jali, you know your son brings this upon himself."

She doesn't respond. She is concentrating on the writing.

a'Sha's yell draws Mald's attention over to the west. Mald nods with approval as he sees a'Sha bend over and grab one of the horses leashes from the back of his own horse while moving at speed.

There was no denying that he was a talented rider.

His father was too.

His jaw clenches at the unwelcome intrusion.

Mald stares up at Godshome, 'ifa Shadelna.

"The flashes should begin tonight," he says.

Jalila hums in agreement at the statement, but doesn't respond.

"I guess this will be a'Sha and a'Jheal's first Festival," Mald continues.

Jalila looks up at her brother and then towards the other planet as well.

"Not a'Jheal's first. He was born a sun's turn before the Festival of 'Ifa Shadelna[1]," she says matter-of-factly.

Mald rolls his eyes.

"That one doesn't count. The first one they will remember is what I mean."

Jalila laughs and turns back to the writing.

---

1. 'Ifa Shadelna ['.i.fa sha.del.na] : Godshome, a name for the wandering planet - lit. "'Ifa" Home, "Shadel" Spirit, "-na" equivalent to English 's

"Has it already been seven turns since my a'Sha was born? Nothing feels further in the past."

Mald nods.

"Time moves faster when we aren't paying attention to it."

The slight sound of sand shifting is the only response he gets.

"His Ul-Fergilna[2] needs work," she says after a few moments of silence as she continues to run her fingers on the rock.

"My nephew needs to focus on doing the task he has been set. Writing and learning a far off tongue must come second." Mald says out loud to no one in particular.

Once again only the desert wind answers him with a soft whistle.

Mald watches a'Sha's dust cloud rise in the distance. He seemed to be doing well rounding up the horses.

Mald smiles.

"Do you remember the Aiwash? When we broke in to let loose those horses? a'Jali?"

Mald's smile drops a bit as he turns to Jalila. He can see her cogs turning.

"So what does it say?" he asks after he realises that she wasn't listening.

"It is a little rhyme I learnt once upon a time," replies Jalila still tracing the wording. "I sang it to him- Still sing it to him. This part is-" she changes to a more melodic tone "-'Val ait'asha vava sjil'."

Mald raises his eyebrows and nods slowly, incomprehension clear on his face.

"It means '*I'm beneath the big crown*'. I think he likes it because crown in Ul-Fergil sounds like his name, Sha."

Mald rolls his eyes.

"Don't mention those people to me. The Fergil. Bastards the lot of them."

---

2. Ul-Fergilna [ul fer.gil.na] : Language of the Fergil - lit. "Ul" Word, "Fergil" People from Fergil, "-na" equivalent to English 's

He rubs his hands as if washing them.

His distaste fades as fast as it came. "They do have strong horses though. And good bowmen too. But they can't beat *us* in speed and range. They would probably need to sit and bathe and wash their hair after every mile. I have to admit though, I regret not taking up that Fergil[3] trader's offer back in the day. Maybe I should try to get my hands on one of their stallions again…" Mald begins to trail off in thought.

"Always the horses," comes Jalila's reply from under her breath.

Mald's train of thought takes a moment to get back to the present.

"Does Ul-Fergil use a' like we do?" he asks.

Jalila cocks her head to one side in curiosity. "Language? Culture? I thought you only cared about their horses," Jalila laughs. "I didn't know you cared about their language too."

Mald shrugs.

Jalila laughs again.

"The closest translation would be 'little' I think. And I don't think they would ever describe each other as little," she says, "even their friends. Especially not their friends. Power is their way of life. They are proud and far from humble."

She pauses thinking.

"Actually," she begins again, "They are very similar to you."

Mald shakes his head.

"Don't do that," he says.

Jalila laughs.

"I won't let you compare us," Mald continues, "We are nothing alike. I am free on the land. They are bound to it. Our strength comes from our freedom. Their's comes from removing freedom."

A moment of silence passes.

A subconscious jerk makes him hold a hand to his abdomen, and to the scar from a war a lifetime ago.

---

3. Fergil [fer.gil] : The name of the Western Eye Empire, People from the River Fergil

They each let the silence swell.

"Now," Jalila says getting to her feet and turning to Mald, "I'm sure you will teach my little Sha to be very strong and very free and to only bath after many, many, *many* miles."

Jalila then turns and looks up to the wandering planet.

"But I will teach him to learn... And to teach. To be someone others can rely on."

She turns to her younger brother.

"Which do you think is more important?"

Mald thinks for a moment.

"As long as he can choose," he says slowly and with a grin. "I guess *that* will be up to him."

SHA

It's past noon as two dozen blue-clad figures and their mounts snake through the desert and dirt towards the east like a blue river through a canyon, following a path only seen and known to them. Around them small yellow and green desert shrubs provide the land its only shade.

Camels and horses hold the younger and weaker 'Ifacho, along with pulling most of their wares. The others follow on foot beside their animals. The travel is slow, but making progress.

Peals of children's laughter ring out from the centre of the pack.

"Stop laughing at me," Sha says holding the side of his head.

He is on top of one of the camels. Every step causes him to wince. On his left and on another camel is Jheal. To Sha's right are Kita and Aunt Talia riding a camel together, daughter in front of her mother. The little girl can't stay still, and her mother is trying desperately to calm her and ignore her at the same time to focus on riding.

The two children on either side of Sha don't do as he commands, and they both continue to laugh at his discomfort.

"I mean honestly a'Sha," says the teenage Diwa from behind

him, "how could you not be jumping at every sound after last night? Especially the rumbling of hooves."

She was old enough to ride her own camel.

"If *I* was allowed to be watching the horses, father would not have been able to sneak up on me at all. I would have seen him coming a mile away. I would have-".

"-I would have done this. I would have done that. I would have done that," Sha mocks as he turns around to face her.

"Well you can't do those things a'Di because *you* are a *girl*. And *girls* can only marry-"

A slap sounds across Sha's face. Diwa has whacked him with her riding whip hard enough to cause a bright red mark to immediately spread over his cheek.

Sha opens and closes his mouth, unable to form words.

Diwa huffs.

As his mind comes back to the present Sha's thoughts turn to rage. He jumps up, still on the saddle, trying to whack Diwa back.

Aunt Talia stops the confrontation short.

"Children!" she shouts commanding their attention. "Do you want me to bring ao'Shiva[1] over here to settle this?"

Both kids freeze.

"No ao'Talia," says Sha with his eyes downcast.

"No Mother," Diwa echoes.

"Good," says Talia.

Sha looks up at her with a mulish glint in his eyes.

"But a'Di started it Auntie," he blurts out unable to keep himself from staying quiet.

Talia jerks forward with fire in her eyes towards Sha. As she does so she accidentally jolts the camel she is on and Kita, in turn, jolts forward uncomfortably.

The little girl squeals and spins around.

"a'Ijd!" she exclaims.

---

1. Ao'Shiva : Ao' + name denotes respect, gendered female

Her mother closes her eyes to calm herself before responding to Kita.

"Shush a'Ki," she says, "you wouldn't be bounced about if you stopped wriggling so much."

She shoots the two older children a scolding look.

"This is your last warning. I will bring your grandmother over."

Sha, Diwa and Jheal each recoil at the threat and take a moment. Sha shudders.

"Listen a'Di," begins Sha again, "everything was fine. I had it all under control. I had almost all the horses back in a group," he looks over his shoulder at Diwa but avoids Talia's glare, "until-".

"-Until you fell off your horse-" interrupts the older boy Jheal still laughing "-and made all of the other horses run away again!"

He is a year older, but roughly the same size and shape as Sha. The two boys aren't brothers, but they look as if they could be.

"Yes a'Jhea. Yes. Stop laughing. It really hurt," says Sha in response.

Jheal tries to contain himself but can't hold it in very well.

"An 'Ifacho[2] who can't ride a horse," he blurts out.

Talia takes notice of the conversation and shakes her head.

"Sha, you are almost a man. You are fine. Maybe you wouldn't have fallen off of the horse if you were a bit *more* careful, and a bit *less* of a show-off. Doing tricks and showing off gets horsemen killed. If you fall off a horse in battle you will die. Real men- real 'Ifacho don't show-off."

The conversation's humour wears off.

"Yes, ao'Talia," is all Sha can respond.

Talia nods her head. Then she turns to face front where her husband and Jalila are deep in conversation.

Sensing this conversation is over, and not wanting to be the

---

2. 'Ifacho ['.i.fa.cho] : Our Tribespeople's name – lit. "'Ifa" home, "cho" negative, or homeless

centre of his cousin's laughter, Sha speeds up to get to the front where his mother and uncle are.

His cheeks burn as he passes by Jheal and Kita. Jheal appears to ignore him, but Sha meets his eyes briefly.

Jheal turns away giggling.

Kita on the other hand sticks her tongue out at him as he is riding away.

Did they all think it was so easy to gather all those horses? That he could just run and gather the reins? It was all just so unfair. Uncle Mald would never have done that to *his* son.

A few paces out Sha can just make out Diwa muttering under her breath.

"I hate him."

Sha pretends not to hear but his eyes sting.

"Don't speak like that Diwa. He is our family as much as any of us are," comes Talia's response.

Diwa lets out an audible sigh of annoyance that Sha just catches at the edge of his hearing. His shoulders hunch up a little.

The terrain, Sha notices, is getting rockier as he moves up the train. There was more shrubbery, more life around, but that made traversing it more treacherous as any missteps could be disastrous. Despite this the 'Ifacho caravan train takes the dirt and rocks and sand in stride. The hidden path winds up and down some minor hills, but it is a route well travelled and well known by them.

Quickly enough Sha reaches his mother, and as he does he hangs back to catch the edge of her and Mald's conversation.

The two are atop their own camels, and riding with Mald's silver-white mare beside him.

"-always feel like I am getting sick when I come here, you know." Mald spits, "And for Tijjikauz to not even have a proper stables for his horse. Does he even have any proper horsemen left? Just how far has he fallen since even the last festival. Let alone since the retaking."

Jalila waves her arm behind herself.

"That's why he wants this-" She almost can't speak the word out loud, "-marriage. He needs our house. Our horse. He always has. You told me this. His control of this ocean of sand rests on our horse."

A bird squawks over-head as the words settle. Sha looks up expecting a red-crested Maithane, but instead sees a large, ugly, water bird.

He cocks his head to the side. He had only ever heard about them.

Jalila spots the bird as well.

"He is going to ask for our help to take the south isn't he Mald?"

Mald adjusts a strap on his saddle, but doesn't answer.

"What will your answer be?"

"It should be no. Our alliance was only ever temporary. But I don't know what he will do if I refuse," Mald responds after a few moments.

He gazes up at the blue sky. Sha follows his gaze upwards. Nothing but a few birds.

A wind from the East picks up and puts the hairs on Sha's arms on edge, the smell of the sea winkles his nose.

"All I know is that I will not join if I see those black sails from the East," Mald says, ice behind his words. "They make me feel more sick than the city itself."

JALILA

THE CONVERSATION HOLDS its natural lull after Mald's declaration.

Jalila stares at her brother. He has one hand unconsciously over the left side of his belly. She shudders at the recollection of his telling of how he got it.

Damn those Terkizcho for where they lead us, and for what they are.

As bad as her time amongst the people of the West Eye were- they would never have- *could* never have come up with the cruelty and chaos that those Terkizcho black sails sow in the East Eye.

Thankfully the ocean of sand here, and the mountains of the north, blocked their path across.

Pray to the Shadel that they never find a way to bring those ships across the bridge of the world.

"Why do you think you are getting sick, Uncle? What are the Black Sails?"

a'Sha's voice pipes up from behind the pair and breaks her sombre recollection.

Mald and Jalila turn to face him.

"Hello there a'Sha," Mald says. "These cities... They are sick places. Dangerous, and dirty, and-".

Jalila cuts in.

"What your uncle means to say is-." She pauses, taking a moment to think about what she is going to say. "Well, do you remember when you were sick last turn?"

a'Sha nods his head.

"Do you remember how bad it made you feel?"

a'Sha nods his head again.

"It's a bit like that. The feeling of it at least," she says.

A gust of wind blows in from the East bringing with it the smell of the sea, and more... there was the hint of an odd smell mixed in with the sea air.

Must be the city.

"We are here" says Mald.

The three reach the crest of a hill at the head of the caravan. Stretched out and in front of them they see the twin cities on the shore, the bustling northern Kiraj'it'Jalila[1] and to the south the broken and crumbling Parfi'at[2].

The only gap left to close now was the open space between the hilltop and the cities.

Jalila looks back to her son with an expectant smile. He paces forward and angles his camel between the two adults. He is looking on wide-eyed. He had seen the sea before, and he had seen smaller towns before, but this was something else for him.

The Twin Cities weren't quite cities. They looked more like two large towns sewn together, but her son's rapture was delightful all the same. The walls surrounding Kiraj'it'Jalila were crumbling in places but upkept and strong. Below it lay the second ruined Parfi'at, deserted and left to rubble, a sign of past wars without the will to repair them. Where Kiraj'it'Jalila was re-inhabited and restored, Parfi'at was not.

---

1. Kiraj'it'Jalila [ki.rai.it.ja.li.la] : Tower by the Sea, or city on the shore – lit. "Kiraj" tower/fortress, "'it'" next to, "Jalila" sea/shore
2. Parfi'at [par.fi.'.at] : First Stable, or Old Horse Stables – lit. "Par" first/old/before, "Fi'at" stables

Between the city walls and the tribespeople lay an open plain that merged into a shanty town closer to the city. To Jalila, it resembled water leaking from a dam. It was built haphazardly and without planning wherever space could be found.

Jalila turns her focus back towards her son. She follows his eyes as they dart excitedly around the city. First he lingers on the main street of Kiraj'it'Jalila inside of the city walls, filled with bazaar stands and indistinguishable movement from up here. Then, following along the main street with his eyes, a'Sha finds the port, and almost gasps when his eyes settle on a single large warship sitting squat in the harbour.

A shock courses up Jalila's spine and into her fingertips as she sees the warship.

She turns to Mald wild-eyed and sees that he is also staring at it. She can see the cogs turning in his head.

She turns back to it. Even from here she could just make out its masthead. Her eyes were good, but it was her memory and imagination that filled in the details. But she wasn't sure.

It would have to have a crying-face as its masthead.

The sails would be black. Now they were furled, making the colour unclear. They couldn't be black, could they?

Surely she couldn't trust her senses from this distance. They would never have it this close to the city.

It can't be.

After a moment Mald turns to her, and shakes his head.

She lets out a small sigh in relief, yet her heart won't stop its manic drumming in her chest.

She focuses on the cities again to calm herself down. All in all the twin cities had the look of a once major trading port that had been destroyed and then haphazardly been moved back into because money could be made, and life must be lived.

Despite trying to ignore the ship, her eyes kept being drawn to it.

This was nothing compared to the Great City of the Western Eye. The thought sprung from the dark deep of her memories.

Instinctively she reaches out to find her a'Sha. To her relief, he is still exactly where she left him staring in wonder. Her chest heaves a deep sigh.

Old wounds had a habit of aching during the quiet moments.

"a'Sha-" Jalila says.

He doesn't respond.

"a'Sha," she repeats louder.

Again he doesn't respond.

Jalila leans over to him and turns his head gently towards her own.

She speaks softly, "it is beautiful isn't it?"

a'Sha nods his head, and they both look upon the city ahead.

"It is very…" Jalila continues. "Pretty… it is pretty. But like how you felt sick, a city feels sick. It makes people sick. It affects how people think, how they act. It forces people to stay still. To obey men with power and the will to use it. It causes men to hoard, to become jealous, and to build walls and dig holes to feel safe. It causes them to fight and die even if they don't have to or want to, and ultimately it forces them back into its roots to feed the soil."

Mald decides to jump into the conversation.

"Which is why we roam," he says smiling. "We own the land without having to put up any walls, we have air. Earth. Water. Shadel."

a'Sha, looking out at the town and the town's walls, tilts his head.

"But it looks like they own that land, no arrow or camel or horse could ever get into those walls."

Mald laughs and nods.

"It does look like that, doesn't it."

He puts his hand up to his chin and rubs it.

"Well," he says making a show of thinking out loud. "-Well, here is a test for you then. If you can figure out how *we*, you and I and all of us, could raid a place like that. A place with a town before itself to make any cavalry useless, and with walls to the sky-"

a'Sha looks from Mald and back to the town. He responds excitedly without letting him finish.

"Have you ever raided Kiraj, Uncle?"

Jalila looks on at Mald with a restrained smile, but an edge of annoyance flares in her eyes. She is almost daring him to say yes.

"Once upon a time," Mald responds amiably and patiently.

He glances at his sister with a little mischievous gleam in his eye.

"But that was a long time ago," he says shrugging. "We have an agreement now with the Dirauj[3] Tijjikauz, we make this desert his and his overlord's. Besides we wouldn't be foolish enough to charge straight from the front, our losses would be too great. Even if we are known as a desert storm."

He raises his arms and wiggles his fingers at a'Sha, "unknown and unpredictable... coming from the desert like white and blue lightning."

a'Sha giggles.

Mald smiles and leans over to tap his white mare affectionately.

a'Sha turns from his uncle to Jalila to confirm. She nods.

"Back to the question. If you can tell me how to raid a place like this..." Mald points towards Kiraj. He comes to a decision with a chuckle.

"I'll allow you to join me on a raid."

a'Sha swings towards him with wide-eyed disbelief.

"Really Uncle? Really?"

Mald nods and laughs. "Yeah, we'll raid a city with your plan!"

Jalila catches Mald's eyes and shoots him a murderous look. She turns quickly to her son.

"He is playing with you a'Sha. You *both* know that you have to be older. You haven't seen enough festivals just yet. You are too

---

3. Dirauj [di.rauw] : Shah, King – lit. "dirauj" crowned man

young. Besides you won't be raiding *Kiraj* anytime soon as long as our agreement stands."

a'Sha ignores her, focusing only on Mald.

"Okay! Let me think about it!"

Jalila taps her son with her riding stick. He swings around.

"Pay attention to me a'Sha. He is playing with you. You can think up a plan but you won't be raiding anytime soon. You won't be ready to go out until you are older. The most important thing is knowing when to fight and when not to."

She gives Mald another frosty look, and then turns back to her son.

"A raid isn't worth it if you die."

a'Sha pouts at her.

He turns to Mald, who winks back at him and laughs.

Suddenly smiling, a'Sha turns and rides off at pace to go talk to his cousins behind him.

Mald tries to hide his good humour as he catches Jalila's eye.

He quickly looks away as if something very interesting were happening some distance off towards the desert.

Jalila clicks her tongue disapprovingly.

MALD

DON'T LOOK AT HER, she might actually hurt you this time.

From behind Mald is suddenly pushed and, despite having seemingly been born in a saddle, he almost falls off of his camel.

Regaining his composure he looks towards his attacker, "Hey! Careful! I nearly fell off!"

Jalila's face has darkened.

"How irresponsible! After what happened less-than-two nights ago you can even think of raiding? After what happened to my son? You absolute pig! He will not be raiding until he is of age Mald."

Mald tries to push her back but can't reach her.

"What happened last night happens," he says. "It's how we live. It's how we survive. You know this. This is our way, and if you try to keep him too sheltered he will eventually just do it anyway but without your protection."

"And you will get him hurt if you keep acting like a child," Jalila retorts.

"Besides," continues Mald ignoring her last comment, "He is more mature than you realise."

Mald strokes his camel's neck. Then he reaches down to grab something from one of his satchels.

It's a small sapphire-encrusted dagger.

"Here," he says tossing the dagger to Jalila.

She catches it with an easy swipe of the air.

Jalila inspects it, unsure of what Mald was meaning. Mald sees the realisation dawn on her.

"This... This is a'Sha's dagger. He came to me crying that he had lost it during the raid. Where did you find it?"

"I found it embedded in his mare that was on top of him," he replies.

Jalila doesn't quite understand.

"He loved that horse. He wouldn't have stabbed her himself would he? Did the attackers steal the knife from him and stab the horse? That can't be right."

Mald looks ahead towards the city.

"I'm not quite sure of the why. Maybe he dropped his knife, they found it and out of the kindness of their shadowed hearts they wanted to give it back to us as a message. Maybe they stole it from him, but then why wouldn't they have just killed him? Besides that he would never have dropped the faijh willingly or unwittingly."

His grip on his horse's reins tighten.

"They were here to kill and steal our horses," Mald says with conviction. "Without our horse, we could no longer be the horsemen of the eastern 'Ifacho and our hold on the land weakens... we become less valuable to the Dirauj."

He sighs and relaxes his hands.

"But how did they get a'Sha's knife? And if they could take it from him, why did they not kill him? Why were our horses the focus, and not just us? If they wanted to wipe us out, they should have just come at us in force rather than sneaking around our outriders. Something is happening here that I don't quite understand."

He looks to Jalila, but finds no answers.

"But it was merely a raid little brother," she says. "A suicidal raid I will grant. But small and contained. We still have the majority of our horses back at the Oasis. Unless there was another attack back there, then this was merely bad luck, and not enough to weaken any of our strength."

Suddenly he laughs, his serious demeanour evaporating.

"That is true. Maybe I merely imagine daggers in the dark. But sometimes I swear I can feel them poking me also. For now there is no need to worry a'Jali. I will always keep a'Sha, and you, and Talia, and a'Jhea, and the girls, and Shiva, and everyone here safe."

He spreads his arms out wide. "Why else are we here?"

Jalila rolls her eyes.

"*ao*'Shiva," she says mocking Talia's voice. "Shiva doesn't need protecting from anyone. Our mother could conquer the world with just her voice."

"Careful mocking my wife," Mald chides her. "*You* are scary, but *Talia* could make my life hell."

Jalila chuckles.

"Talia isn't some kitten that needs you to protect her, she gives just as good as she gets."

They both laugh and turn around to spot their mother and Talia, who are seemingly deep in conversation.

Kita is still squirming in front of Talia, causing all kinds of distractions. Shiva, not to be beaten by her grandchild, is clearly the one commanding Talia's attention and doing all the talking.

Talia respectfully nods her head in agreement at some comment that Mald couldn't hear.

Mald smiles. It took a long time for her to figure out, but Talia eventually learned to just listen and nod. With Shiva she knew she couldn't really get a word in anyway.

Jalila laughs under her breath as a thought comes to her.

"I wonder if Mother even knows what Talia's voice sounds like."

Mald responds with a laugh. "I don't think she has ever let her speak."

Behind his mother and wife comes a crash.

Mald and Jalila follow the sound to its source. Ilatr, a surprisingly good-humoured man, is looking quite unsure of himself at this very moment as he has his ear chatted off by a'Sha.

Mald sees it and laughs.

"Our a'Sha is definitely related to Shiva. Ever since he learnt to speak he has never stopped. I don't think Ilatr has ever been able to quite handle it."

Jalila laughs also.

"Not many can handle my a'Sha."

They both take pleasure in watching Ilatr squirm under a'Sha's childish commanding tone.

"He's a good man you know," Mald says after a few moments, and as he says that, Ilatr shows a'Sha his sabre.

Jalila sighs, but allows herself to smile as well.

"He is a good man," she says.

a'Sha reaches out to touch the sword.

With a whimper he pulls back his hand quickly.

Ilatr laughs as a'Sha begins sucking his finger with a sour expression on his face.

"Have you come to a decision about his proposal?" Asks Mald.

"Maybe I will, maybe I won't," Jalila responds quickly, her cheeks burning.

She shrugs.

"So. No. I haven't decided yet."

Mald follows her gaze as it falls on Diwa.

A shadow falls across his sister's face.

Jalila turns back towards the city.

"You know I don't like it. I don't like it at all. I remember my own-", she stops herself short. "She hasn't got a choice. Every woman should have a choice. And she is too young. Even I wasn't that young when I had to."

Mald looks back towards his eldest daughter Diwa, and can't help but notice that despite being a young woman now, she was still a girl who had only barely seen two festivals.

He turns back to face Jalila.

"I hate it. I don't want it. But we have no choice either. She is my first and eldest... and it was a condition of our agreement from the retaking. You know as well as I do that there is no other way. I can't fight them all. And we won't survive in the middle a'Jali."

With the use of her name Jalila nods her head and stares forward.

Mald continues.

"I fear losing this place- *Our* place in the world. Our homes. Even what happened last night. Nobody would have dared unless they smelt blood... When did we lose our grasp?"

Mald sighs.

"The Lions of the East Eye and of the West Eye are closing in on each other again. The Southern Lion died long ago. They are just slowly bleeding out until someone else takes their place. They may have some fight left in them, but as they are they won't survive... And we are being forced further and further into the centre of our ocean. Into the middle... We hold the east as if chained to it. And if that chain comes loose? I dread to think. Now is more important than ever to solidify our allies. And Tijjikauz is our ally. We have none other than him... and the Eastern Lion that is *his* master."

"And if our *ally* and his master use the ships again brother?"

Jalila's question cuts through Mald.

"What kind of masters does Tijjikauz have," Jalila continues, "that you then also must bow to?"

"I bow to no one Jalila."

Mald's tone is deathly serious.

"Yet you offer your daughter to him," Jalila responds flatly. "You may claim that your knees are stiff, but Tijjikauz will force you to bow. The alternative to subservience is death in the land of the Terkizcho."

The Hourglass That Swallows You

"Death..." A thought shocks its way through his mind, and it shows on his face, "...or joining with the Fergilna[1]."

He stops himself quickly. That name leads to a dark, avoided corner of his mind.

Mald re-centres himself mentally.

"-No. We will not die. I will not allow it. We need to solidify our allies."

The sound of the camel's hooves mix with the horses' hooves to make a soft clip-clomp as they move through the sand.

"You've fought everyone before," says Jalila quietly, but the conversation is done.

Silence hangs in the air, the siblings each in their own thoughts.

The Twin cities get bigger with every step.

"I'm going to get everybody ready," Jalila says after a while.

She reins her camel around and makes her way back to the rest of the group.

"We need them." Mald responds to the shadel invisible around him.

He turns and sees his eldest daughter with the rest of his tribe.

"We need them."

He repeats under his breath as he turns back around alone at the head of his pack.

"But shadels curse it, my knees do feel very stiff."

---

1. Fergilna [fer.gil.na] : 'Ifacho affiliated with the Fergil – lit. "fergil" People of the Fergil, "na" equivalent to English 's, or owned by

JALILA

THE CARAVAN TRAIN makes its way through the ruined outskirts of the twin cities. Around them the hastily, yet somehow also old, mud and brick and wooden houses have been erected in the shanty town outside the city.

Even from here, the outskirts of Kiraj'it'Jalila, the tower by the sea that gives the town its name dominates the skyline. The short slightly overhanging parapets gave the ancient sandstone tower a feeling of age, as if time had begun slowly blowing the tower outwards in all directions.

Jalila catches herself gazing up at it and slowly her thoughts stumble back into the present.

She turns and finds Diwa, while around her the other children are laughing and playing. Diwa's perpetual teenage frown turns to a pout as she stares at the ground too involved in her own thoughts.

To Jalila she resembled a Maithane bird amongst crows, lonely even amongst her own family.

a'Sha's eyes meet her own for a split-second.

Jalila responds with a smile.

a'Sha only half registers it as he is intensely focused on something in his hands. Then, either registering the meeting of the eyes or feeling her gaze on him -Jalila couldn't tell- he looks back up with a mischievous glint in his eye.

He hides himself briefly, then suddenly shows himself and smiles at her with a wide grin, palms open and empty.

Jalila glares at him.

She starts to rein in towards him.

Before she can get anywhere near; a'Sha, a'Jhea and a'Ki keep their distance and start playing somewhere further down the line.

Jalila begins to follow but catches sight of Diwa again.

Jalila pauses and sighs.

She slows and corrects her course to make way towards Diwa instead.

"Shadel caged your thoughts?" Jalila asks softly as she reaches her.

Diwa nods her head slightly and looks away, over towards the old destroyed houses and walls.

Anywhere but the present.

Silence passes between them.

A breeze is picking up, bringing with it the smell of sea salt and alcohol. The walls and the crowds are getting thicker and thicker as the group continues forwards into the town. People are celebrating, their loud voices and drunken songs carrying on the wind.

"Sounds like the festivities have already started," says Jalila.

She is met with no response from Diwa.

Jalila considers the festival around her. Every seven turns the Planet of Spirits comes to meet ours. Here in Kiraj, when Godshome comes to meet ours, it was a time for festivities; a time waited upon for celebrations and weddings for it was thought to bring good luck.

Such is not the case in all places she has been in her time alive. The Western Eye viewed it as sacred. They would put out candles to light up the dark corners of their cities to mark the passing of each day until the shadel would leave on another pilgrimage away into the darkness.

She remembered it was a solemn time. Morose. Quiet.

She much preferred a celebration to a mourning.

"You know the 'Ifa Shadelna festival is a good time for it," she says coming back to the present, "very lucky."

Diwa grunts in response but doesn't say anything. The continued lack of a verbal response causes Jalila to sigh.

A slight ripple runs through the tribespeople as they reach the wooden gates, flanked on either side by large stone lions, that lead to the city proper.

A wave of the hand from the guards lets them all through and into the centre of town. The centre of town is different from the wood and mud and brick of the shanty town. The stone walls that surround them have turned yellow-brown with the passage of time.

The sound of the camel's and horses' hooves turn from a soft thud to a sharp clack as the tribespeople pass the gates; cobbled stone and dirt signify the main streets.

The main street is wide enough to allow six horses side by side to pass through, but because of the festivities and the haphazardly set-up stalls and bazaars the tribespeople are forced either to travel in single file or dismount.

They dismount to group up in pairs.

Diwa and Jalila dismount with the group.

Diwa begins walking forward alone.

With a bit of a jump Jalila speeds up to catch up.

City folk, who would usually stare at the rare sight of the nomads within their walls instead ignore them, more focused on the celebration and music around them.

Despite that Jalila feels eyes upon her, and not just from the sellers around them, but from the darkened windows and shady corners of the alleyways branching from this main street.

Jalila ignores them as best she can and tries to start up a conversation with Diwa again.

"You were a'Sha's age last time you saw the flashes weren't you?"

No response.

Another moment of silence.

Jalila clicks her tongue in frustration, but tries again.

"They say this is the time that the Shadel come from Godshome-" she points up to the wandering planet, "to visit us... To visit old loved ones. To check up on us. To give their blessings and to curse us."

Another silent moment passes.

She closes her eyes, clenching and unclenching her jaw.

They are reaching near the central market place and all around they are getting more and more constricted.

Large yellow-beaked seagulls squawk overhead.

Jalila can sense the eyes starting to stare upon them. All around more and more people are coming out of their homes to look at the tribesmen as they continue down the central street. Most are drunk. Some see and ignore. Others shield and hide.

Let them hide.

Despite the sentiment Jalila found herself keeping an eye out for the slightest movement.

"I remember when your Grandfather and Mald presented me with the bridal jewellery," she says turning towards Diwa. "Looking back, it wasn't so bad... the wedding I mean. The black tent... the eclipse, and the flashes. I remember-".

Jalila reaches out to hold Diwa's hand.

With a sudden jolt Diwa bats her aunt's hand away from her own.

"-I don't care Auntie!" She shouts. "I don't care. Just leave me alone!"

With tears in her eyes Diwa turns away and quickly makes her way to the back of the group.

Jalila is too stunned to move. She stares at Diwa's back as she walks away unsure of what just happened.

She quickly comes back to her senses with a fire in her mouth.

"Don't you dare speak to me like that!" Jalila shouts.

Diwa speeds up.

Seemingly ignored, Jalila's face turns a shade of crimson. She starts to follow until she feels someone grabbing her arm. She spins to see who would dare grab her arm, only to find Talia looking at her square in the eyes and gently shaking her head.

"Stop," Talia says sadly, but firmly. "Just leave it."

Unable to properly give voice to her frustration, Jalila turns back to Diwa and opens her mouth as if to shout again, but stops herself.

Instead she turns back around to Talia.

"She is scared…" says Talia. "But that is no reason for her to be rude. Let me deal with her later."

Jalila frowns, but also nods, accepting the explanation.

With a wave of her hand Talia signals for them to keep moving.

Jalila casts her eyes to the sky and follows closely behind.

As they walk, the streets suddenly open up to a rabbit's warren of a market square. The market pulsed with the energy of hundreds of people, it was packed with stalls and bazaars that formed an almost complete enclosure around and above.

People heckled, shouted and bought and sold all manner of items here. Sweet leaf and silk from the east, furs from the north and gems and salt from the south.

All manner of goods were bought and sold here.

Sitting high above, visible through the sometimes colourful, sometimes tan overhangs, was the tower that gave the city its name.

"Come. Let's help Mother unpack," says Talia as they follow their group towards a relative open space.

Some of the group ahead has already started setting up the caravans, tents and stalls. Near the corner of the square, in a lone patch of sunlight is the matriarch of the tribe, mother of Jalila th'ana[1] Kali and Mald th'ana Kali. Shiva th'ana Mi'athauz.

She led the unpacking and setting up effort with an iron fist

---

1. Th'ana [th.a.na] : born of, from, lit. "th'a" – born, "na" equivalent to English 's, or owned by

despite her aged stature. Truly she was the closest thing to a queen of the desert that the desert would allow.

Within the comings and goings of the city folk and the tribespeople, Jalila can just make out Mald talking to a'Sha and a'Jhea who are nodding and laughing in response.

Mald wore a mischievous look on his face, much like his nephew usually does.

The family resemblance ran strong.

Mald points over to a building nearby, a tavern. The two boy's turn to follow his gaze. Then they both look at each other wide-eyed.

They all begin to move towards it until Shiva's voice cuts through the sound of the city.

"a'Mald. What are you and those boys doing?"

All three stop in their tracks.

Despite the words, it wasn't a question.

"Don't think you are too old to get a clip across your ear!"

The two boys look at each other unsure and then look at Mald, who shakes his head, in this Shiva over-ruled him.

"Get over there and help unpack," she commands Mald.

"Yes ao'Shiva" is his meek response.

He, rather like a big kid, commands the rest of his men to help set up the wares.

Shiva turns her eyes to the remaining boys, who seem to shrink under her gaze.

"a'Jheal, a'Sha don't just look at me with a silly look across your faces. Help him. Now. Go, go. When you finish your chores you can explore," Shiva says.

The boys murmur a soft yes to her.

She nods. "Good. Go."

"-But you aren't to leave the market place!" She adds as an afterthought. "And no going near the harbour!"

Her order is absolute and she knows it.

She continues to direct all the men and women of her tribe with a ship captain's roughness and, red-faced or not, all the boys fall in line regardless of age, rank or position.

She spots Jalila and Talia staring at the whole situation.

"Shadel take me–" Jalila begins to say as she attempts to turn but can't get away in time.

"Daughters you can help me here. And where is a'Diwa?"

"She is near the back Mother," says Jalila turning back around slowly.

Shiva nods and turns to Talia.

"Go grab your daughter and come back quickly. I want to get everything out of here, and hopefully buy the dowry jewellery and wedding cloth before the shadel–" she points up at Godshome as she says the word "–come."

"Yes, ao'Shiva," Talia responds and goes off.

Jalila rolls her eyes, and mouths a mock *yes, ao'Shiva*.

Luckily Shiva doesn't notice Jalila doing it.

"See," Shiva begins, "that is a woman who shows some respect for her mother."

She directs this jab at Jalila, who keeps her face like stone.

"Now help me with this knot, my fingers aren't what they used to be..."

Jalila very quietly sighs, but walks over to the tent that Shiva has begun untying and helps nonetheless. They continue to unpack their wares with only the occasional shout from Shiva as if she had eyes in the back of her head.

SHA

SHA IS LEADING Jheal around the bustling market place. They walk in and out of the shadows cast by the faux ceiling.

Smoke makes the air musky, and sand and dust hang at eye level. The smell of cardamom, cumin and smoke from heated coals mix together within the spice markets; incense and other unique smells Sha can't place fill his head and nostrils.

Sha enthusiastically points to a trader demonstrating how to breathe smoke from a large heated water pipe to a crowd of people. The trader's eyes look bloodshot and red, his teeth yellowed.

Jheal points to a woman filling a small leather sack with spice, sweet cane and sweet leaf from the east.

Each boy turns to point one thing out after another. One of them points in one direction, then another points out something else, then the other points out something else, over and over.

Time flies when it is ignored.

"a'Sha, here," calls out a deep voice from a sun-spot some distance off.

Sha turns to the sound and recognises Ilatr's voice. Without realising he and Jheal must have wandered in a big loop around the central market place.

Sha opens his mouth as if to respond, but doesn't, instead his eyes glint with mischievous intent. He pretends not to hear and lightly grasps Jheal's arm hastening them onwards and towards the shadows.

"Boys!" Shiva's voice calling out now, "Ilatr called for you."

Jheal slows at his grandmother's voice, nervous, and pulls back but Sha urges him on forwards.

"Hey! Get back here!"

Shiva's voice calls out louder and more forcefully. The boys giggle, half in fear, half in glee and retreat quickly into the dark spaces of the market and out of the reach of Shiva.

Out of breath they come across the tavern near the edge of the market place.

Sha smiles broadly.

"This is the place Mald was talking about wasn't it?" He says.

Jheal looks over his shoulder for any potential followers. Satisfied that they are not being followed, he turns back around and towards the tavern.

"Yeah it must be."

The tavern is a squat two stories, with makeshift tables inside and out. People sit wherever they can find a seat, on window sills, barrels, even on the floor on deep red and brown carpets. Alcohol in all forms and in all manner of vessels are being used.

The festivities have gotten the entire city drunk. Sha can see men and women like a river flowing in and out and all around him into and out of the tavern and streets.

"We are going to get into big trouble when ao'Shiva gets a hold on us," Jheal says as he puts his hand onto Sha's shoulder, "especially if we go any further-".

A shout interrupts Jheal's plea.

From the shadow of the tavern a drunken sailor is tossed out of the doors by a hulking, grimy bouncer. The bouncer's hair was left long on top, but tied into a rough ball. But below that his head was completely shaved on either side.

It was odd and unlike any hair cut that Sha had seen before. The men of his people, and even the traders would either grow their hair out long or shave it close.

The bouncer rubs his hands causing his veins to bulge and crisscross his tanned biceps and forearms.

Staring, Sha couldn't help but notice a dark drawing on his right forearm of two crescent moons on top of each other with a cross running through the centre.

The drawing causes a flutter of recognition within Sha. He had seen that symbol before, somewhere, but he couldn't place it.

The bouncer walks over to the sailor, bends down and wipes his hands on the sailor's jerkin. Then he stalks back into the tavern.

"Listen," says Sha turning to Jheal, "Shiva gets mad at me anyway. I'd be hung as a lamb the same as for a sheep as she would say. She doesn't scare me."

Jheal furrows his brows in disbelief at Sha's bravado.

"So if I'm going to get into trouble whatever I do," Sha continues, "I might as well do whatever I want. *Free to roam*."

Sha turns back to the tavern.

The drunken sailor is still lying slumped on the ground where he was thrown. A few tables down, an older, scarred and scruffy-looking sailor gets up and walks slowly over to him. He glances to the left and then over to the right. Satisfied he kicks the fallen sailor lightly with his foot.

The drunken sailor doesn't wake up, or even stir. The only sign of life he projects is an unconscious grunt. The older sailor looks around again. No signs of complaint. He whistles to call some men over.

"Come on a'Jhea," Sha says dragging Jheal towards the table where the older sailor was sitting, and where he left his drink unattended. "I want to try a drink."

"I really don't think we should," says Jheal as he looks around nervously, "We should get back before they catch us. Or before we get into trouble. This place feels dangerous. Maybe they won't be too mad we ran *if* we say sorry."

"Stop being such a baby," Sha responds continuing forward.

Despite his objections Jheal follows.

The older sailor's men get to the passed-out sailor and begin ruthlessly searching his pockets. The leader walks over to the sailor's right forearm and rips open his sleeve. No mark, no tattoo. He nods and signals to his men, who drag the passed-out sailor by the legs to a nearby cart.

Sha watches the man being dragged away as he walks to the unattended table.

By the side of the cart, looking towards the market is a well-built man with a trident beard.

Momentarily the sun catches on the officer's sword, blinding Sha. He puts his hand up to block the glare.

The officer turns to greet the older sailor with a cat's grin. Sha notices two inverted 'V's', one larger than the other, are engraved at the base of the blade. They looked similar to the bouncer's tattoo.

The boys watch the exchange with a horrified fascination as they walk. The older sailor and the man with the trident beard exchange some golden coins as the older sailor's men hoist the drunken man unsanctimoniously onto the cart.

Sha turns around to refocus on the older sailor's temporarily abandoned drink, but Jheal can't turn his eyes away from the scene.

"a'Sha," he says slowly, "did they- did they just... buy that man?"

Sha reaches out to grab the tankard.

Hearing no response Jheal turns to Sha.

"What do you think just happened over there-".

Suddenly Jheal lets out a startled gasp.

Before Sha can react his hand is caught reaching towards the drink. Sha jumps as he lets out a sharp intake of air. He spins towards his captor.

And time stands still.

The Hourglass That Swallows You

Jalila stares back at him.

Sha couldn't find his breath, it was stuck somewhere between his throat and his chest.

Jalila speaks slowly, "To answer your question, a'Jhea. There is a war coming, and that Terkizcho[1] Officer," she points to the man with the trident beard, "has just bought some poor soul to fight in it."

Jheal's mouth hangs open in shock, not so much at the words but at the fact that Jalila has caught them.

Sha, on the other hand, is trying to speak, but any words that do escape are incoherent.

His mother drags him to her with an iron grip and slaps him across the face.

His cheek burns as he feels tears stream down his face.

"Did ao'Shiva not tell you to stay in the market?" Jalila says barely holding back the anger in her voice.

"I was a'ijd, I was. We are still in the market-".

Another slap sounds around the outside of the tavern as Jalila slaps her son again.

Sha tries desperately to squirm away but his mother holds firm.

"Don't talk back!" She says, her patience vanishing into the air. "You won't get out of this one a'Sha. Disobeying your Grandmother. Running off here of all places. This place is dangerous at the best of times for us. We should have left you back in the Oasis."

Sha hunkers over sobbing.

Jalila turns on Jheal.

"-And you. Him-" she nods her head towards Sha "-I can understand. But I expected better from you a'Jheal. You have a more sensible head on your shoulders. Speak up more."

You can almost see the fire coming out of her mouth as she breathes.

---

1. Terkizcho [ter.kiz.cho] : The name for the Eastern Eye Empire's people – lit. "Terkiz" to speak, "cho" negative, or mute

"You will both follow. *Now*."

The command is absolute.

She turns to walk back to the stalls, but the boys don't move.

Sha is still completely startled and Jheal is frozen in place.

In frustration Jalila drags Sha alongside her.

"Come a'Jheal," she says. "*Now*."

Jalila stalks off with Sha beside her. Jheal follows closely behind, too scared to disobey.

Sha looks back over his shoulder to the table. He sees the older sailor slump back down happily with his new money in his hand. In celebration of his sudden windfall he takes a long swig of his drink, and calls out for another.

Sha turns his eyes forward again.

"Mother, I was just exploring, I wasn't going to go too far-" Sha begins but is cut off.

"Stop it. Now. You are not getting out of this. ao'Shiva is going to have a field-day with you when I tell her about you both."

His eyes go wide as he realises the trouble he is going to be in.

"No- no, please don't," Sha says beginning to squirm again. "Please a'ijd, please-".

Jheal's eyes go wide as well, he doesn't want to get in trouble either.

Jalila's grip on Sha's arm gets tighter but he keeps squirming, trying to find a way to free himself.

"Keep it up a'Sha and you'll have more to worry about than just Shiva," threatens Jalila as they walk back into the shadows.

MALD

MALD RUBS HIS HANDS TOGETHER, and stops himself abruptly mid-motion with a wince. The rope burn he acquired from setting up his market tent still burned.

From somewhere in front of him a yell rises above the market.

He quickly spots the source and sees a sailor leading a chain-gang through the market place. A glint from the sailor's sword reveals that he is a Terkizcho Naval Officer, and Mald confirms it by spotting the double crescent moon tattoo'ed on his right forearm.

If Mald had to guess he would guess that the men in the chain-gang were convicts- or at least men declared as convicts- and were to be put to service for the Eastern Lion.

It was a cruel fate. They might not know it yet but it was a coin-flip whether they would become part of the vanguard, men to be pushed through the meat-grinder, or worse, a harbour for the weaponised miasma.

Despite the rope-burn he rubs his hands together without realising.

A slight cough from behind him pulls him back to the present.

"Did the Eastern Lion take *complete* control over this place while we were tending the sand?" Mald asks the cough behind him.

"So it's true then," says Ilatr ignoring the question as he moves to Mald's side, "akal'Tijjikauz and The Great Dirauj are gearing up to reclaim the south."

He points towards the convicts.

Mald nods and sighs.

"It seems to be," he says.

"Truly, he is bringing the best of the best."

"You know well enough that he doesn't need the best of the best," says Mald. He gives a short, mirthless laugh "Just enough of a man to push forward and to die. Whether that be to the spear at his front or by the spear to his back. Tijjikauz's overlord demands ground, regardless of the cost of it."

Mald stares at the continuing chain-gang before turning to his second-in-command.

"Our horse is too valuable to be fodder... but then he knows that. He asks of us to be his sword in the desert and his trader's shield. He dare not lose us for fear of losing his grasp on the ocean of sand. And his overlord would merely replace him if he were to. His power currently lies in *our* ties together and as long as he doesn't demand *this* of us," Mald gestures towards the men in chains, "then our relationship will stand".

From the dark of a side street nearby emerges a skinny horse with a gaunt-looking rider perched on top. The rider is wearing the drab brown-stone coloured uniform recognisable as one of the town's Guardsmen. Without realising, the guardsman wanders in front of the chain-gang, blocking their progress.

"Behold," says Ilatr, "the head of Tijjikauz's horsemen has come to inspect the new recruits."

"You jest," responds Mald, "but I think that *that* truly is the greatest horseman Tijjikauz has to offer. With such a man it's no wonder the Northern Terkizcho want Tijjikauz's riders on their side."

Mald lets out a grim laugh at his own joke, while Ilatr's eyes stay focused on the scene unfolding in front of them.

The chain-gang pauses with a jolt as the lead man fails to avoid the horse in front of him.

Angrily the Terkizcho masters try to wave the horseman away.

Seeing an opportunity one of the men in chains screams and tries to bolt. He makes it a few steps before the chains on his ankles and hands force him backwards. He falls awkwardly, dragging another prisoner to his knees.

Shouts from the prisoners draw the attention of the crowd. A few members of the public crane their necks towards the scene but spin just as quickly back away, not wanting any part of it.

The prisoners are quickly silenced and the one who tried to bolt is knocked back down to the ground with a hard hit from the hilt of the sailor's short sword.

The sailor doesn't stop with just one hit.

Yells of pain ring out through the street with each dull bloody squelch.

The Guardsman's horse's nostrils flare as he whinnies in fear at the smell of blood.

Mald clicks his teeth, these guardsmen's horses haven't been bred or trained for warfare. They were too skittish and the guardsman had no idea how to handle him.

The horse rears up, throwing his rider off.

He hits the ground with a hard thwack.

A hoof lands within a hand's width to his knee. The guardsman panics and rolls away, narrowly avoiding the hooves hitting the ground as the horse leaps and kicks the air.

Walking over to the rider on the ground, the Naval Officer draws his sword.

He pauses, looking beyond the guard on the ground and down the side street. He yells something Mald can't make out and takes a step back.

Another guardsman appears from the side street on foot. He looks older, wiser, more engaged with the situation. He strides towards the horse to calm it.

More riders, more City Guardsmen, appear as if from the walls themselves until finally, from the rear, a greying Captain of the Guard emerges from the street on horseback.

It had surely been a while since Mald were last here. He couldn't recognise the man.

The two groups, Terkizcho and Guardsmen, face off.

Apparently Kiraj *still* had some of that old 'Ifacho blood in them. That was a good sign at least.

Maybe the Eastern Lion hasn't completely removed the children of the shadow and taken hold of the city yet. Perhaps Tijjikauz still has some autonomy left.

If there *was* hope, it would come from the people here.

Sensing the tension the Naval Officer quickly sheaths his sword and opens his arms towards the Captain as a sign of truce, to show he had no ill intention.

The Captain of the Guard nods and dismounts gracefully.

They meet in the centre and begin to speak with hushed voices.

The gaunt rider scrambles to his feet and moves to take over from the wiser guard who calmed his horse. He doesn't meet his gaze but instead tries to pat the horse's nose.

He is met with a short sharp snap of the mare's teeth.

After a few moments of quick discussion the two leaders come to a visible decision to allow each other to continue. They nod at each other, and the Terkizcho Naval Officer turns back to his guards.

The Captain of the Guard wears an unreadable expression as he stares at the man's back before turning back to his own men.

Ilatr shrugs.

"I guess the show is over," he says.

The men in chains head off to the east down the main road and towards the port.

"Awful riders. Bad horsemen. And worse warriors. Only the old have any sort of grace, but no energy. That's why they stay in the city and we are needed out there," Mald comments watching the rider try to remount his horse.

He makes it up on the third attempt. Finally back on top of his horse, he leads the men to continue on towards the initial direction that they were going. In the back some of the guardsmen laugh to each other.

The Captain follows bringing up the rear.

Before the group disappears from view the Captain of the Guard turns and catches Mald's eyes. Mald matches his stare until he is out of view.

Old blood indeed.

He sighs, "We have spent too long here already. This place is dry brush, and I think the tinder is about to fly. Even the air," he coughs, "-the smell of this place is making me sick."

Ilatr chuckles, looks at Mald and responds, "Like a rock you are. So strong."

Mald ignores that comment. Instead his eyes happen upon his sister holding a'Sha and a'Jhea by the ears.

"Kiraj is undergoing a transformation," Mald says slowly, thinking as he speaks. "And I'm coming to the conclusion that Tijjikauz can't control the outcome. He will come and ask for our help as he has always done, to bind the old 'Ifacho blood to him and to his lord... but I think-... I'm not sure what my answer will be."

Ilatr continues to look at Mald, but he takes a moment to collect his thoughts before responding.

"We have committed ourselves to a path. The wedding forges our union in blood and by iron. He will expect us to follow where he wills. To deny his request if it comes to it... That is a dangerous and hidden path, fu'aitauz. We follow where you lead akal'Mald, but know neither Tijjikauz nor The Terkizcho Dirauj will like that, there *will* be a backlash."

The market bustles around them, it's getting closer to the time of the eclipse.

"My offer is my most precious jewel..." he shuffles his feet uncomfortably, "and a promise to hold the sand for him. In exchange all I ask is that we won't have to repeat the turning of the hourglass. I won't risk our people to be as his vanguard again."

Ilatr lightly grasps the Eastern Mace by his side.

"Aye," he says softly.

a'Sha's childish shouting echoes off of the sandstone walls around them.

"Let me go! I won't go to her. I won't. No. No! Leave me alone."

Ilatr turns and changes the subject. He nods towards the oncoming Jalila and children.

"Looks like a'Sha has gotten your boy into trouble again."

Mald laughs and his face changes happily from his previous serious demeanour.

"They are little trouble-makers. Like all boys."

"That they are," Ilatr responds. "I hope I live long enough to see how he raids one day."

a'Sha is still shouting and struggling to free himself.

By contrast a'Jheal is holding Jalila's hand to his ear relatively calmly and submissively.

Mald replies, "If a'Sha continues fighting us, Shiva will gut him before we can ever see him raid."

Jalila and the boys are getting ever closer.

Ilatr looks back at Mald and laughs, "I was talking about *your* son. But a'Sha is a little fighter also. Far, far too wild though. And he never stops talking or arguing long enough to think."

Ilatr waves a hand to Jalila. She doesn't initially see him as she is focused on forcing her son to stay still.

a'Jhea glances up at his Aunt and tenses.

Out of the corner of his mouth Ilatr says, "akal, a'Jhea is about to run."

Ilatr was right.

a'Jhea has been waiting for this momentary distraction.

Mald nods at Ilatr.

As Jalila looks up to Ilatr, a'Jheal bursts out of her grasp.

Mald has already started moving.

Jalila shouts and swings around to a'Jheal who is already at full pace running away from her. The distraction causes her to loosen her grasp on a'Sha.

He also bursts out of her grasp and starts off at full pace in the opposite direction.

"I hate her!" He screams behind himself, "I won't let you take me to her!"

Mald grasps a'Jheal's arm with an iron grasp, stopping the boy suddenly with a jerk. He hadn't noticed him until it was too late, and looking up at his father he knows Mald has him caught.

"What have you both been doing, boy?" Mald asks without emotion.

Jalila shouts at the speeding a'Sha, who is very quickly making some distance between them both. He is running at full tilt towards the harbour.

Jalila looks towards Mald for help.

"Don't kill him until I get back," she shouts as she sees that Mald has a'Jheal caught. "I want my turn for them both."

Mald grins, malice reaching the corners of his smile, as he nods to confirm.

His son squirms, but can't escape his father's grasp.

Jalila turns back around and begins to run as fast as she can after a'Sha.

"ao'Jali, I'll help!" Ilatr calls after her as he starts to follow.

Mald grabs hold of a'Jheal by the scruff of his neck, and continues to stare down the street in the direction Ilatr and Jalila ran off.

a'Jheal shuffles a bit in his grasp.

Mald tightens his grip, but doesn't look down.

After Ilatr disappears from view, Mald turns and drags his son to the rest of his people without even a glance down towards him.

As he reaches their dark stalls he hands off his son to Talia without a word.

From the corner of his eye he sees Shiva walk towards them with wrath in her eyes.

"Those little dogs."

Shiva says.

"When I get my hands on that little brat I'm going to-".

Mald cuts her off.

"Mother. Stop. When we catch him do your worst. But *after* we catch him. Right now this place is dangerous."

His eyes catch the darkness in the eyes of the laughing revellers around him.

"First things first we need to find him before he gets hurt."

"Too much of his bloody father in him," Shiva says under her breath.

Mald's face turns dark and he looks his mother square in the eyes.

Shiva quickly stops muttering.

"We need to find him before it gets dark," Mald says.

He looks around at his people. With a whistle and a gesture he begins to round up his people to start to search for a'Sha.

SHA

Sha runs at full speed towards the ocean and the harbour. His eyes are streaming as he catches fleeting glances back over his shoulder.

No one is following him... so far.

He spins back around and is met by something unyieldingly solid. He flies backwards, leg-over-head, hitting the ground hard, winding him.

Sitting up to catch his breath he looks up to see what he hit into and stares straight at a large drunken man that he mistook for a wall.

The man turns slowly towards the small child, his head swaying slightly. He squints. With a sound somewhere between a hiccup and a burp he turns back around to his group. As he does he accidentally sloshes his drink over Sha.

Sha scurries to his feet while the man utters something incomprehensible. Standing he scuttles a few steps back from the looming drunk man, who turns back around to him.

The man grunts, laughs and passes Sha his drink as he cracks a crooked smile.

Sha hesitantly grasps the drink unsure of what to do with it.

The man raises his fist to his face as a gesture for him to drink.

Slowly Sha does.

It's completely foul. With barely a gulp he splutters the drink to the ground and begins to cough.

The big man laughs uproariously.

"a'Sha!"

His mother's shout rests lightly on the air.

Sha, still coughing, hears the distant shouting of his name. He looks back over his shoulder.

"a'Sha!"

He couldn't see her, but the calling is definitely getting closer.

Time to go.

He hands the drunk man back his drink, and with an awkward bow takes off at speed towards the harbour.

The fear on his face turns slowly to enjoyment as he runs as fast as he can from the big man and his group. The cooler sea air filters through his nose with the smell of salt and heat, cleansing the smell of the city as it flows through it.

It was a welcome relief from the near stifling haze.

Sha snakes his way through the crowds like a cat looking for a vole between tall blades of grass. All around him are people, more people all together than he had ever seen before, and he is enjoying the pressing of the crowd.

A wild smile begins to creep over his face. With the wind and the sounds and the smells whirling around him, dipping and dodging between people he feels untouchable, and free.

He catches a glance upwards. Overhead the sky is beginning to darken with the eclipse of Godshome.

Quickly he faces forward, so as to not hit into anyone else. Streaming past him to his left and right are people selling wares, trinkets and fabrics. He felt a strange surge of pride as he looks at the fabrics. Despite the high costs none were as beautiful as his tribe's blues.

His ears ring with the cacophony of musicians as they beat out asynchronous beats and rhythms over one another, a far cry from the silence of the desert sands.

Men and women of all ages are drinking, laughing, and dancing along the main street making the most of this once-every-seven-years festival. But in the shadows, out of sight, in alleyways, and around each corner Sha can see drunken men falling about themselves or slumped over. Beside them are groups of Terkizcho, binding them or dragging them away.

Sha slows to catch his breath and within moments finds himself being jostled around by some unaware dancers who push and shove him without realising. With a few quick steps backwards he escapes them to a street corner.

Free from the crowd he hunches over and looks around. To his left is an alleyway stretching between two sandstone buildings.

The alleyway was empty, but still an unease rippled up the back of his spine. The shadowed walls around him felt as if they were enclosing.

He quickly turns from it back towards the crowd until a clink, metal on stone, draws him back to the dark.

He peers down into the dark of the alleyway.

A group of men are talking to a Terkizcho officer, while on the ground beside them lays a broken figure hidden by shadow.

Sha catches the eye of the largest of the group of men.

Where the others in the group were dogs he was a wolf.

Sha quickly swings back around the corner to escape his gaze.

He swallows, and despite his nerves screaming at him to walk away, slowly peers around the corner again.

With a quick sigh of relief the wolf man has turned back to the others.

This time Sha is sure he isn't noticed.

The officer flashes a few coins from his purse.

"*Skirdherng*," he says.

The language was foreign, but Sha knew it as the language of the Terkizcho. It felt spiky.

Sha didn't know what it meant, but the large wolfish man seems to be receptive. He nods and replies too softly for Sha to make out.

Suddenly from behind he is pressed against the wall beside him by the crowd.

As quickly as it came he feels the pressure release off of him and lets out a gasp. With the rush of air comes a sickly sweet smell from the woman who had just collapsed by him. As she gets up, her drink sloshes out of her remarkably upright mug.

The splash narrowly misses his head. He can smell that disgusting liquid as it drips by his face. The woman gets up and spins around with a stumble in her walk.

"Oh sorry love. Are you hurt?" she asks in a rougher form of his tongue.

Sha shakes his head at her.

She looks him up and down with a sorry look on her face.

"Here," she says, flipping a small silver coin to his feet.

He looks at the coin on the floor without moving before looking back up at her. With a quick flash of a smile, she spins around and as quickly as she came she disappears into the street dancing.

Sha picks up the coin slowly, feeling the edges and turning it around in his hands. It was different from the ones he commonly saw. With a finger he traces out the head with a set of laurels around it and furrows his brow.

He flips it to the other side and traces out what looks like a dead tree with two concentric circles around it.

A noise from the alleyway behind him drags his attention away from the coin. He peers back around the corner and into the shadows.

The situation had changed, but the Terkizcho officer hadn't yet realised. The men with the wolfish man have the officer surrounded.

The officer realises his mistake too late.

"I'll not be a little mouse amongst the bloated rats on that death ship of yours," says the leader, in the same rough tongue as the lady before, "...but I will take the Dirauj's coin from him."

Steel flashes out from behind the Terkizcho, and a knife slides into the officer's back. The officer opens his mouth to scream but his face is quickly muzzled by the leader with one hand, while the other plunges a second knife into his front.

Sha backs away with shock spreading across his face. He covers his face with his hand and stumbles.

In the distance he can just pick out his mother's shout.

Her shout pulls him back to himself. He starts to panic.

"Shadel take me," he says.

His feet are heavy, and he feels petrified.

"Move Sha, just move," he says to himself.

As if sensing Sha's fear, the wolfish man looks up and locks eyes with him. Bent over the dying, squirming officer is the ghoulish figure of his murderer, holding him by the shirt.

Sha's eyes go wide.

The wolfish man gets to his feet, pulling the man up.

Every sense in Sha's head screams at him to bolt.

"Move- Move- Move!" He shouts at himself.

He turns and forces his way through the crowd.

Fear gets the better of him and he turns his head back to spot his pursuers.

Instead he sees the body of the Terkizcho hit the ground with a heavy thud. The Terkizcho stares dead-eyed towards Sha while blood trickles out of the corner of his mouth.

Sha spins and runs with all the strength and speed he could muster.

Behind him he could hear the angry shouting of the wolf men of Kiraj who killed the officer. He glances back to see them forcibly moving people aside as they give chase.

Emerging from the crowd, Sha sees a group of local sailors drinking on a few barrels. From one to another they are passing around jugs of fermented alcohol while chatting and laughing to some women in front of them.

If he hadn't experienced guard duty with his own tribe he would have taken them as regular sailors, but their cheer and ease belied their official capacity. They were guarding the main road towards the ocean, even if only half-heartedly, more focused as they are on the women in front of them.

Sha approaches the group quickly but with a soft step. The hairs on the back of his neck standing on edge.

He has to get past this group. The consequence of letting those wolves get him would be too great.

Then, as if a gift from the shadel, one of the women grab a sailor's hand with a giggle and lead him a little way away from the others. The other sailors and women laugh and cheer, rising to dance themselves.

It's now or never.

As quickly and quietly as he could manage Sha runs past them in the direction of the ocean.

He hears a shout from behind him and the blood drains from his face. No use looking back now, just go.

Go.

Then to his relief he hears the wolves shouting at the sailors and the women.

They must have been stopped.

Sha doesn't look back but continues to run towards the sea.

SHA

SHA ROUNDS a deserted corner at a brisk pace.

He had barely made it past the sailors and that wolf man's group, and in the shadows he leans back against a wall to catch his breath.

Before he allows his breathing to settle he makes certain the men aren't following him.

The alleyway he had paused at was silent, another tunnel in this rat's nest of a city. He could hear the faint beat of the city festival echoed on the walls over his heavy and ragged breathing.

His heart felt like it was going to burst as it fought to bring him back to calm.

He couldn't figure out why they had pursued him as much as they had. He was a child of the 'Ifacho, he had felt danger before- had run and hid from dangerous men before- but they were something else, it was as if they wanted him.

And he couldn't figure out why. They couldn't have recognised him.

With some effort he forces himself back to the now and turns to look where all his running has gotten him.

The alley frames his vision. On either side of him he can feel the dark sandy buildings encroaching upon him, and so he moves towards the light in the centre.

The view as he emerges is unlike anything he has ever seen.

Sha stands, chest still heaving, gazing in wonder at the slow enclosing eclipse of Godshome and its mirror on the wine-dark sea, framed within and by the harbour.

Prying his gaze to the right he spots a few small, narrow long boats moored to the jetties jutting up through the water.

His eyes drag over the harbour and, as if pulled and held, land on the crying mast head of the large Terkizcho warship he could see as they were riding in.

Up close he can almost hear the figurehead's siren song, and in response Shiva's voice telling him to stay away.

The thought spurs his curiosity even more.

He buries the morbid curiosity deep for the moment as he stays still to watch the eclipse.

With each second that passes, the sky and Sha's entire world is getting darker and the shadows more ruby.

Words on the tip of his tongue leave Sha at a loss for words.

The wind whistles over the small harbour, carrying with it the impossibly far away sounds of the festival.

Sha can smell- taste even- the salt on the incoming sea air, but with it is something strange. A smell that is familiar but that he can't quite place.

It starts to burn his nostrils. It smells... rotten.

As soon as it touches his senses it glides away with the breeze.

The world gets darker and darker.

A brilliant flash of light suddenly shines and burns out over Godshome. Sha blinks up at it, his pupils going wide at the sudden shift in brightness.

What was it?

Shadel?

Or something... else?

Another shine and fade over the horizon, bigger, longer this time. It leaves a fading bright streak in the sky.

A little away from the planet more shines and fades. Within moments a meteor shower suddenly burns up in the sky and crosses from over the sea leaving a trail of fire and light.

Yet as soon as it came it disappears into the West and over the desert.

Silence.

Sha continues to stare at the course of that falling star, expecting to see more, but nothing comes.

That odd smell from the sea pulls him out of the sky. The more it lingers the more he feels as if he can recognise it, but just can't put his finger on it.

Under his feet he suddenly feels a rumble. It was short and sharp. Like the ripple of a pebble hitting the water but much, much bigger.

As quickly as it came it fades, and the silence of the sea takes over.

His mother's call cuts through the moment, but, thankfully, she still sounded like she was a far way off. Sha looks around to see where it came from.

With his focus pulled from the sky and the sea, the eery stillness of the harbour begins to gnaw at him. He turns back around to look left and right down the harbour.

There was no movement anywhere.

His gaze returns to the empty and shadowy piers and jetties. Pillars like scarecrows cast long cross shaped shadows towards him.

Then a disorienting realisation dawns on him.

It was deathly silent, save for the lapping of waves and the groan of wood against wave.

He was alone.

What happened to the festivities? Did they not extend this far?

It is a far cry from the rambunctious partying in the main square and no one- not even any dock workers or fishermen- are anywhere to be seen.

Only the shadows and the echoes of life.

Sha turns to look back up the way he came, he hadn't realised it while he was running but he must have taken a few extra turns to get here.

Looking up and down again, the realisation that he didn't recognise the alleyway hits him.

His nostrils flare again. That smell again. He coughs and pulls his shirt up to his nose to use as a mask.

Another call from his mother. Her voice is getting closer. Sha can't make out the words but he can tell by her tone that she is angry.

"Good," he mumbles under his breath, "She should be angry." His voice is shaky, despite his angry confidence.

Then he hears Ilatr's voice, the echo causes it to be as shrill and tinny as his mother's.

He feels his heart sink. This was going a lot further than he thought it would go. He is going to be in a lot of trouble if they catch him now.

When they catch me I'll be in a lot of trouble anyway. It won't matter if I turn myself in or not. As Shiva says, hung for a sheep as a lamb.

Sha looks towards the warship.

There.

That doesn't look like it will go anywhere for a while.

He can hide in there.

He nods as if to reassure himself and looks around the ominous warship.

There doesn't seem to be anyone there, and there are lots of places to hide, but a feeling deep from the pit of his stomach is telling him to look elsewhere.

Sha forces the feeling down.

He hears his mother's voice again catching on the wind. It was much closer now. She is almost here.

I'll hide close by.

I just won't go too near it.

With his mind made up he quickly takes off towards the pier and the warship's berth.

The loading and unloading of the warship seems to have halted. Everyone must be at the festival as he can't spot a single soul around him.

To his left and right the pier is filled with old mouldy-looking barrels and fly-covered wagons as he approaches the tall, dark ship.

Sha wrinkles his nose, that smell is stronger here.

He slows down.

It seems to be coming from somewhere around here.

Sha runs his fingers over some of the barrels as he moves past them. They feel splintery, rough and old.

With a quick yelp he quickly recoils his finger in pain and pops his finger into his mouth.

Then after a second he spits out a tiny piece of wood and continues to suck his finger.

As he wanders quickly down the pier, over to his lefthand side, the dark ship looms over him, just out of reach. The bottom of the ship, the part he could see at least, looks black... sticky.

He looks up and shudders at the crying-face figurehead. While it stares back at him with cold, black eyes.

He feels the need to back away from it and takes a step back. He loses his footing staring at her and barely stops himself from falling.

Not just his stomach, but all of his senses are screaming at him to get away.

His mother's voice silences his senses.

He glances towards the alleyway which he came from before ducking and hiding behind a few of the unloaded barrels.

Slowly he raises his head above the barrel to spy towards the entrance.

Up by the alleyway bursts out his mother with her black hair and blue scarf fluttering behind her. She slumps forwards as she reaches the mouth of the harbour to catch her breath before looking around wildly from side to side.

She must be really mad.

"a'Sha!" she calls out.

There is something in her tone that Sha had never heard in her voice before.

She walks down the dirt and wooden stairs moving closer to the berth calling out his name.

"a'Sha!" she shouts out again, "a'Sh-". She coughs, cutting herself off.

She puts the crook of her arm to her nose and mouth.

"a'Sha! Please!" her voice breaks.

Sha watches her, unable to figure out quite what was in her voice. It made him uneasy.

Very hesitantly, very slowly he begins to stand up.

Jalila reaches the bottom of the berth.

"a'Sha where are you!?" Sha slows his ascent. This tone he could recognise more readily.

She sounds angry.

But that crack, that breaking in her voice is still... there.

The tall, lithe figure of Ilatr comes into view. Sha hadn't fully heard him before, as focused as he was on his mother.

Jalila turns as she hears Ilatr calling out for Sha behind her.

Sha ducks back down when he hears his name. It's safer here than facing the consequences of Shiva and his Mother.

Ilatr approaches Jalila quickly. They speak for a moment, but Sha can't hear what they are saying.

Then without warning they both look in the direction of Sha.

Sha quickly hides deeper in the berth near the gangplank.

He takes a deep breath... and peaks his head back over to continue to spy on the two.

He exhales quickly.

They didn't see me.

The Hourglass That Swallows You

He sees her nod up the berth towards where he is hiding. She waves over the harbour itself, directing Ilatr to continue across the harbour.

Ilatr hesitates.

He reaches out and holds onto Jalila's arm and shakes his head at her, a plead for her not to move closer to the ship.

Jalila jerks away from his grip and scolds him.

Sha winces with empathy.

Ilatr looks down to the ground and breathes out a long, hard breath. Then he looks her in the eye and says something that Sha can't hear.

With a quick turn he walks southwards down the harbour, calling out Sha's name.

Sha turns his focus back to his mother. She is getting closer to his hiding place, searching each nook and cranny.

If she kept coming this way like this she would be able to see me. He takes a few cat-like steps backwards.

A bright light catches the corner of his eye. He looks up in the direction of it.

Sha blinks.

Way up above him in the sky the other world, known to him as Shadelna, Godshome, begins to eclipse the sun.

As he opens his eyes the world around him flashes in a brilliant green. A light source coming from the shine of the eclipse, something like the first rays of dawn, turn everything around him a bright green, a shade of which he has never seen before.

Disorientated, Sha throws his hands up to shade his eyes as he looks all around him. Then back up towards the eclipse.

As quickly as it came it disappears.

Sha takes a step backwards to get a better view of the eclipse, just in case it flashes again. As he does his belt-scarf catches onto a loose nail and falls to the pier without him noticing.

Around him the Godshome eclipse casts long shadows.

His foot touches the gangplank up onto the ship.

He hadn't realised just how far backwards he had moved. He spins around to it.

He panics as he notices he is out in the open. He could get caught if he stayed out here. He quickly runs up the gangplank and onto the ship.

The plank creaks loudly with each step as he runs up it. It's only five or six paces long, but it is steep and as he is trying to be as stealthy as possible he is out of breath as he reaches the top of it.

Reaching the top he ducks down and quickly surveys the ship. The ship is large, and piled with boxes covered by long, dark sheets. At the back is a well-worn platform with a large rectangular rudder sticking out.

He turns to look towards the front of the ship. Maybe it was a trick of the eyes but it seemed to stretch all the way towards the town, bowing slightly upwards at the end, and at that end he could just make out the iron hair of the figure head at the front.

He had barely a moment to take it all in before hearing his mother shouting his name on the pier.

Sha moves cat-like behind the wooden railing on the warship to peer down at her. He raises his head to peer down over the edge of the ship.

His eye catches a belt-scarf left discarded on the gangplank.

He looks down quickly at his waist.

Shadel take it.

That *was* his.

He ducks down quickly cursing his mistake under his breath.

Then he peers back over the edge of the ship to spot his mother.

He sees her as she reaches his old hiding place.

She looked distraught, furious and scared all at once.

"a'Sha!" she shouts, looking around.

"Please, a'Sha. Please come out."

Her eyes drop to the ground. She is almost in tears.

She rubs her eyes and gulps, raising her hand to her mouth.

The Hourglass That Swallows You

The hairs on the back of Sha's neck raise. He swallows back a feeling of guilt and starts to stand up.

Then stops abruptly.

Jalila has stopped moving. She is focused on something on the ground. Sha follows her gaze and sees his belt-scarf. He looks back at her.

Within a few quick paces she gets to it and delicately picks it up.

Sha ducks down again. Breathing heavily.

She'll find me. She'll-

-Silver, quicker than a blink, flashes in and out of the corner of his vision.

His dark hair whispers across his face followed by a cutting breeze.

He hears a dull thud followed by a metallic rattle knock the wood next to him.

Warm liquid sprays onto Sha's arm and face.

Sha can't react. It takes all of his effort to tilt his head and look down.

He sees a rat lying on its side beside him, with a short, stubby knife jutting out from its side.

Sha can't move.

His mind is blank, but he is very aware that his back is towards the middle of the boat. And that is not where it should be.

Like a rushing tide his body untenses.

He opens his mouth to scream, but before a sound can escape a big, sweaty hand blocks his voice and covers his mouth. That smell invades his nostrils, the man's hands stank of the stuff.

Despite the fear and panic, it suddenly clicks how and where he knows that smell from. It's the same smell as from those dead horses, the smell of old blood and decay.

He struggles desperately to free himself, kicking and squirming, but he can't do much against a fully grown man. With a grunt from the man, Sha feels his feet get lifted off the ground as he is dragged away from the railing.

With all of his struggling he is just able to look up and glimpse his captor.

His eyes focus on the man's trident beard.

Sha's eyes go wide with tears and fear.

He catches a glimpse of his mother through the railing, down below on the berth.

She can't hear him.

She doesn't know.

She turns away with his belt-scarf in her arms.

Sha tries to call out to her, but the officer holds him tighter, any sound of struggle is snuffed out by the overpowering man.

Fears causes something to stir in Sha. His instincts take over.

He bites down hard on the exposed, disgusting skin of the man's hand.

The officer shouts out in pain and loosens his grip.

Sensing the weakness Sha breaks out of his grasp.

They separate. Sha is thrown down roughly, while the officer takes a step back, more concerned with the bite than the child.

Sha sees blood begin to trickle down the man's hand.

"Ulghe zasuulanga?" The officer says quietly, panic infecting his voice.

Sha doesn't understand, but the man's voice scares him.

Sha steps backwards towards the gangplank.

"Ulghe Zasuulanga?"

Again the words are meaningless to him. Sha doesn't know this language, but he feels the panic rising.

A gull squarks angrily overhead, and a crow responds with its own angry caw.

The officer comes to his senses. He is furious, his eyes are bloodshot.

The officer shouts out, "Ulghe zasuulanga!?"

Sha spins around and runs towards the gangplank.

"Mother!" Sha screams his voice breaking.

JALILA

"He has to be around here somewhere," Jalila mutters under her breath, "but please a'Sha... please don't be anywhere near here."

Her cheeks are red with exertion. Her eyes are red from the strain of searching every shadowy corner around her. Not to mention that overwhelming stench of decay is making her eyes water.

Mald was wrong, this smell, the look of this ship...

She didn't want to believe it... but this could very well be a Black Ship, even without the black sail.

The look and feel of this ship is just as was described from the war stories Mald and her father told of the East Eye, by the vast swamp lands.

Two decks, the lower held nothing but corpses. The top, the weapon to launch them. Or so she had been told. She had thought it was a just embellishment by her brother.

If this is one, then this is the first one she has ever truly seen.

The Western Eye had no weapons like this.

And they had this ship of death barely contained, guarded by little more than a handful of drunken sailors and local rat-catchers, moored *here* on the edge of *our* ocean of sand.

Even the heat of the desert would have difficulty purifying the darkness if this was released.

No. Nothing good will come after this.

The thought sent a shiver up her spine.

Her a'Sha can't be here. Despite the finality of the thought, it was more hope than reason.

She turns from the ship, and as she does her foot gets caught on something soft. Turning back around she bends down.

No.

She picks it up to inspect it further.

It is.

It's her a'Sha's scarf.

She looks back up at the ship… and shakes her head.

No, he wouldn't be so stupid as to go up there.

She looks over the port and begins to walk back.

"Mother!"

Her son's wild scream rings out over the empty harbour.

Jalila stops dead in her tracks.

Her heart stops.

She swings around to stare up the gangplank and ship.

"No," she says to herself, her voice ice; the hairs on the back of her neck stand on edge.

At the top of the gangplank, with Godshome casting long ink-black shadows towards her, appears a'Sha moving as fast as he can. Blood is running down his face and onto his shirt. He gets one solid footfall onto the gangplank before his arm is caught from behind.

With a yelp he is dragged back by a dark figure with a trident-shaped beard. She recognises it instantly as a mark of an Terkizcho Officer.

Her feet are moving before her brain kicks in.

Above her, on the ship, she can hear struggling.

As if by magic her hunting knife appears in her hand. She is running on pure instinct.

She reaches the top of the gangplank and sees the Terkizcho. He is threatening the boy with a long knife.

She can't make out the words, but she knows it as the ul'Terkizcho, the language of the mute.

Her son is ineffectually punching, biting and kicking to be freed but the little boy can't match the strength of the grown man.

"Let go of my son!" Jalila shouts out, loud and fast.

The sailor looks up and spins her son around in response. He puts his blade to a'Sha's neck roughly.

Jalila looks from the blade cutting a'Sha's neck to the officer, and snarls.

Her son is still struggling even as his blood is drawn.

Jalila isn't distraught anymore, the feeling has been replaced by an ice-cold rage.

Her voice is steady, and on the outside she appears calm, despite the maelstrom within her.

"Let. Him. Go." She says as she flips the knife in her hand to a reverse fighting grip.

Slowly she hunkers down and brings up her arms in a fighting stance.

The officer growls at her and tightens his grip on her son.

"Aitshii, kaaghe kigheul rdermat! Tul ookaagh kingeetheme phamas. Gedje dguullasga. Vhit aivhini djhaasul, aivhezi dheubak."

The foreign words fall deaf on Jalila's ears.

The air is still.

Neither of them move.

Jalila can't pry her eyes away from the long knife cutting into her son's neck, but her body moves with purpose. She edges further onto the boat's deck. Slowly and softly but steady.

"Let my son go," she repeats calmly.

No movement again.

He might not understand what I'm saying.

But he will understand my blade.

As if responding to her thought the officer digs his blade deeper into her a'Sha.

"*Putan! Aivhezi dheubak. Tul ookaagh kingeetheme phamas.*"

He is getting louder and angrier with each word.

Crows and gulls caw loudly. A rare meal might soon be theirs.

The heat causes Jalila's arms to begin to bead with sweat.

The air feels stagnant.

Salt and rot burn her nostrils and throat.

She takes another step forward. Her feet find the deck and stop. Stillness.

Water softly sloshes against the side of the Black Ship.

"*Rdermat!*" The officer shouts.

Exasperated he throws the sobbing a'Sha who falls hard to the deck, momentarily stunned.

Jalila breathes a quick sigh of relief, but it is short-lived.

The officer levels his blade directly at her.

Jalila speaks without taking an eye off of the officer.

"Sha get up."

The officer is statue-still. His chest is moving up and down deeply.

He is taking big deep breaths, as if he were calming himself for something.

She tightens her grip on the blade.

She takes a few tentative steps towards a'Sha, but her eyes never leave the sailor. She is watching him as carefully as she can as she moves to her son.

Jalila reaches a'Sha within a few steps.

She reaches a hand down to him, but her hand can't find him.

She looks down-

-And a white light suddenly flashes over the right side of her vision.

The pain comes within a heartbeat.

Jalila cries out and puts a hand up to her right eye as the officer's long knife clatters to the floor.

She stumbles.

She had only looked away for a moment to check on her son but in that moment had seen him in shock, trying to speak but only mouthing words.

Jalila tries to open her right eye but can't. She could feel the blood trickle from above her eye and down past her mouth.

She got lucky. Only the butt of the knife hit her above the eye.

Movement ahead flashes her instincts into action.

Within a few paces the officer has drawn his sword, and seeing an opening, springs into an attack.

Despite her readiness she had been caught off guard. She hadn't expected him to toss away his weapon so recklessly and now with his sword drawn, and with only her hunting knife to hand, she is immediately put on the back foot.

With a mighty overhead swing the officer has a weight advantage over Jalila.

She can only block him and deflect as best she can.

"Sha. Run!" shouts Jalila in between breaths.

The officer hits again and again. His strength is overpowering. She can barely hold him off, let alone fight back, and it's clear that if she can't find a way to escape both her and her son will be more ammunition for this ship.

From the corner of her eye she catches a glimpse of a'Sha on the ground squirming backwards watching. His eyes wide open in fright.

The wound on his neck looks as if he were wearing a scarlet scarf. He is making sounds but can't form words.

Jalila is losing this fight.

With a grunt of effort the officer manages to break through her defence and slash across the top of her chest.

She recoils and half falls, half jumps backwards.

The officer looks over to a'Sha, and finds him still on the ground petrified.

He moves in towards him and chops down at the boy as if splitting wood.

Jalila moves fast to block it. She gets under the blow as it falls.

She holds her offhand under her knife to keep it from being dragged down, but can't match his strength.

a'Sha barely moves at all.

One of Jalila's knees slam the wooden ground beneath her.

The officer uses his weight to force the sword inch by inch down towards Jalila's head.

"Sha-" Jalila says through struggling gasps of air as the sword is brought slowly towards her forehead.

"-Please. Get. UP!"

The boy still won't move.

"Sha!" She yells as the blade begins to slowly cut her forehead.

Blood begins to drip as Jalila's head is slowly being cleft in two.

Suddenly, as if the shadel themselves touched the boy, sense is brought back to him. He grabs the Terkizcho long-knife that was left thrown on the deck of the ship as he gets up.

Sha scrambles to his feet and runs towards the gangplank. He turns suddenly to climb up onto one of the large covered wooden machines.

Then without a second thought he leaps at the officer, screaming the word he heard from another officer before, *"Skirdherng!"*

The officer turns, distracted first by the word, and then by the action. By instinct he stops pushing down against Jalila and deflects her son with his off-hand.

a'Sha falls out of the air and onto the deck. He hits the ground hard, wind knocked out of him.

With weight off of her Jalila moves like a snake, and with a swift violent motion runs her blade through the officer's heart.

The officer blinks.

Incomprehension flashes across his face, the question clear in his eyes.

The Hourglass That Swallows You

He stumbles backwards and drops his sword. It hits the ground with a soft clatter.

Jalila runs forwards and wrenches the knife out of the standing man.

The officer falls heavily to the deck spluttering blood.

Breathing heavy Jalila falls to her knees on the deck.

a'Sha scrambles over to her.

She embraces him with open arms and hugs him close.

SHA

IN THE RED-DARK of the eclipse and crying in his mother's arms, Sha can feel the heavy heaving of his mother. He realises, as he begins to feel the world beyond his own heart and head, that he is breathing just as heavily.

He can feel the gentle sway of the sea rocking the boat.

He can feel the course wood on his knees.

He can feel his own warm tears streaming down his face.

"I'm sorry a'ijd, I- I- I'm so sorry- I-".

Jalila holds him closer and tighter, but her arms are shaking.

She feels weak.

Sha is spluttering, mumbling softly but not forming any full words or sentences.

After what feels like an eternity and yet could only have been a few moments, Jalila gently pushes her son away.

She inspects his neck. He winces as she tilts his head up and down.

While she is inspecting him, Sha gets a more full view of her also. He can see the toll that the fighting has taken on her.

Her right eye is swollen shut and bleeding, her forehead has a jagged line cut down the middle of it and the top of her chest has a deep horizontal line going across it.

As she catches what he is doing she smiles at him and kisses his forehead, then holds him closer.

He felt safe in her arms, to him she felt like finding water in the desert, or light on a moonless night.

But they weren't safe.

Not yet.

Not on this ship nor in this city.

Slowly a noise in the dark corners of Sha's hearing begins to grow.

Waves of buzzing followed by a ringing silence.

Scratching, little claws on wood.

More of his senses edge into the corner of his head.

Smells that the sea air can't completely cover, that smell of rot and decay.

The ringing grows.

His nostrils are burning.

His heart skips in his chest, and he swallows hard.

He leans back to try to focus on his mother, but at the edge of his vision he can see little yellow eyes, reflecting the dark sky.

Jalila grabs her dusty red head-scarf and ties it around his neck.

She tightens it.

His neck hurts.

He puts his fingers up to it.

They come away red with his blood.

Sha hadn't realised he was cut.

The scarf is too uncomfortable.

It's too tight.

He squirms and pulls at it.

He gets dizzy. His eyes go cloudy.

"Stop, a'Sha. Don't touch it my little one. Keep it on," says his mother.

Sha looks with clouded eyes at his mother as she tightens the scarf around his neck again.

It hurts.

It's too tight.

His eyes and head drift as he weakly tries to fight her.

Sounds seems to move with his eyes towards wherever he looks. He can hear more of those claws on wood scratching around him.

He turns his head to try to focus on the loudest of it.

And is met by yellow-white eyes, dark irises the size of oceans stare back at him.

Fear courses through him. His fingertips pulse as his nerves fire on all cylinders.

Sha's eyes open wide. He can't take his eyes from the dead officer, and the officer can't stop staring back.

As quickly as she notices, his mother turns his head towards her.

"Sha- a'Sha. Listen to me. I know it hurts, but push and hold here," she places his hand onto the scarf and applies pressure.

"Hey-," she continues, "-hey. Come on, this is okay. You will be alright. Just breathe with me-".

She drags his forehead to lightly touch her's. They both breathe out, and back in.

"You did so well," she says softly to him. "You did so, so well my little crown. My little lion. I love you. Be strong for me and keep this tight around your neck."

Sha tries to respond but no words, no sound at all comes out.

Jalila pushes her son away gently and wraps Sha's own belt-scarf over her bruised and swollen eye.

Then he sees her suddenly wince and tense up. She grits her teeth, whips out her small carving knife and reactively swipes down.

Sha sees a rat's body separate from its head. The head falls from her leg and onto the deck with a low thud.

He sees the rat's blood mix with hers at the wound site.

Jalila dismisses it without a second thought and looks back around the ship as if nothing had happened.

"Come on my a'Sha. We have stayed too long. We need to go," Jalila says softly as she slowly gets to her feet. Her legs shake as she gets up.

Sha digs in deeper to the hug and lets his mother help him up.

His eyes drift again and his head feels like it is swimming.

He coughs, and then whimpers in pain at his throat. His senses are being overpowered. His mouth tastes like metal.

A loud thump behind him, followed by a sharp gasp, spin him and his mother around. His mother instinctively reacts by jumping into a defensive position, and pushing Sha behind her.

Sha peers around her and sees Ilatr standing on the edge of the deck, his mace in hand. The sight of the blue scarf of his tribe almost brought him to tears with relief.

He feels his mother go from tense to relaxed as she breathes a sigh of relief.

Ilatr looks from mother, to son and then to the dead sailor. He lingers on the man with an unreadable expression. Then turns back to the pair with a grimace. The distant recollection of similar scenes crosses his expression and passes as quickly as it comes.

"There will be no one more on this ship whilst here in the port. But that does not mean we can linger. We must get back to the others." Ilatr says looking about the ship, "We cannot be found here."

Sha sees his mother look down at the bite. It looks deep and painful. But she seems to dismiss it; It's just another wound to dress. She puts pressure on the gash then rips a piece of cloth off of her clothing and ties it tightly around it.

The Shadow of Godshome moves off, and begins to light up the world again.

Jalila looks back to Ilatr and nods.

Sha looks up at his mother and then around the ship. She is attempting to shield his eyes, but as the red light starts to brighten up the world again, he can more easily make out what this ship looks like.

Around him are more of those wooden structures. He had heard about these before but had never actually seen them. Uncle called them catapults.

He continues to scan the ship. Near to the topside ladder, but before the backroom quarters are a few bunks. He can see dark shapes lying on them.

Didn't akal'Ilatr say there was no one else on the ship? What about those people?

His heart begins to pump a bit faster.

Why didn't they wake up during the fighting?

They look so peaceful and still.

But something about them is making the hair on the back of his neck stand on edge.

Shadel.

The thought whispers across his mind. Ghosts.

Sha gasps, swallowing in a big gulp of that stale, foul-smelling air that he had almost totally forgotten about during the fight.

He coughs again, the cut on his neck is still bleeding. The violent action of coughing brings tears to his eyes and he whimpers again. He brings his hands up to put more pressure on his neck. Through the tears in his eyes he can still see what made him gasp.

He blinks hard.

None of the men were sleeping. These men are dead.

And they are staring at him.

Their yellowed, dead eyes engulf him as though he were under a canopy of them.

He feels his mother catch him as his vision goes black. She hastily covers his eyes, blocking the Gaze of the Shadel.

"a'Sha," he hears her say from a universe away. "Don't stare at them. These men have taken the walk to 'Ifa Shadelna. They can't hurt you."

Something clicks as she realises why that officer wanted her and Sha off of the ship.

Her legs feel weak, they are trembling.

"The Shadel... have them-", she begins.

Sha can hear footsteps behind his mother's hand.

"They can't hurt you-", she continues.

Sha feels his mother's grip loosen, while Ilatr grabs her arm forcefully.

"We have lingered too long Jalila. This is a black ship. We must go. Now," Ilatr's command is urgent.

Within a couple of steps he pulls her and Sha off of the ship.

Sha begins to breathe heavily. It feels like all of his blood is rushing to his extremities at once. He is tired.

They follow Ilatr's lead until, on the gangplank, Jalila stumbles and grasps at her leg.

Sha grips onto his mother's hand tightly and almost goes down with her, but she manages to keep them both upright.

As a group they get as far away from the black ship as fast as they can.

Around them the harbour continues its second dawn.

MALD

THE SHADOW of Godshome passes over the market place with a raucous cheer from the dancing revellers. Yet Mald and his tribespeople stand apart.

Despite the talk of them being the same people, from the same stock and joined after the falling of the dam in the south many generations ago, Mald couldn't feel more different from these city-dwellers.

Both people believed that 'Ifa Shadelna was the home of the shadel and the home of the gods that created the universe. That the eclipse was the point at which we could just glimpse the majesty of *their* home, of ours also after we take the walk.

Our 'Ifacho, the people who wander, took the opening and the closing of the eclipse as solemn. A time to remember the old ones, and the ones who now won't ever grow old, in quiet contemplation. The people of Kiraj, on the other hand, celebrated the lives of their dead with cheer.

That was but one way of many ways in which they stood opposed. Yet despite their differences they did both believe that this was a time of intense change.

Lost in his thoughts Mald found himself staring at his people from his perch in front of his tent. They were still trading to the drunken city folk, but they were nearly done.

He takes a long swig from the ceramic mug of tea in his hand, it was sweet with a taste of mint. He finishes it and inspects the inside. Then he sighs as he puts it on the ground next to the wooden foundation of the tent.

His fingers trace the wood as they rise over it, inspecting it and the tent. The wood is solid, but it was a trader's tent and set up hastily earlier this day. His fingers find a crack starting to form in the wood from age and use.

Above, near the top of the wood, a large light-brown canopy lay draped over a light wooden skeleton. Its entrance hoisted up by two skinny wooden pillars that allowed the ground beneath to lie in shadow, before a similarly coloured flap led inside.

The tent was meant to keep his people shaded and protected, but not to last forever.

Wind knocks up the bottom flaps of the tent's brown fabric, which whips back with a crack. Mald feels the sea air pick up. It makes the small hair on his arms stand on edge.

There is something on the air. He had been smelling it since coming to Kiraj.

Mald's gaze shifts back over to his people. Shiva is haggling with a couple of young drunk men over the price of some of her sapphire blue fabric. Jheal is scrambling under her feet, making sure he is there at her every beck and call but also out of her arms reach, just in case. He knew when to be subservient when he needed to be.

Mald cracks a smile. It is clear that the men attempting to haggle with Shiva have almost no power in this situation despite being the buyers. They were attempting to buy the sapphire blue fabric, and for that they would pay a hefty price.

The creation of that fabric was one of the most distinctive and highly guarded secrets of his people. Initially the secrets had been known only to the far east, but during the campaign that killed his father, Kali, and made Mald the leader he was today, he had made it his tribe's signature. Now all the lions surrounding him knew his tribe for it.

Not to mention it made his 'Ifacho rich.

Wealth. These men that were being haggled by Shiva were but merchants, trying to resell the fabric further down the line.

No, Shiva wasn't the reason he could sense that something was off. She didn't need any help from him.

He continues his wandering gaze. All over he has his people making trades: for wine, for tea, for that sweetness from over the East Eye sea.

That sweetness causes a stir deep in his mind, but no tangible thoughts.

Mald shifts his gaze again.

He just can't place a finger on it.

His eyes wander over a small herd of horses being lead by a group of the Dirauj's men. He could recognise the horses as Eastern Golden Mares. They were average sized creatures, bred for long journeys across the steppes of the north. A lesser relative of the Western War Horses, but where they lacked in size, they made up for it in stamina.

How odd.

He had only ever seen them during his time in the east. They had a hard time crossing the mountain ridge of the bridge in the north, and they hated crossing the east eye sea. Not to mention they were too meaty to survive the heat of this ocean of sand for too long. Obviously the Dirauj had found a way to bring them over, maybe they were in trade for something?

He would get his answer during the wedding.

He looks up to the retreating eclipse and remembers a voice from his past.

He smiles and looks back towards the mares.

"I think you are right, akal'Kali. They would mix very well with our silvers," he says the thought out loud.

An image of the attack a few nights ago flashes across his eyes, his dead horses. Silver and Gold-.

"I haven't thought about that man for a long time," says Shiva's voice in front of him.

He looks up, and smiles. She moves quietly for an old woman. The distraction leaves his thoughts by the wayside.

"Even after all this time I still miss him, Mother," he says softly. Shiva grunts and looks away.

"He took you... and the others... away to fight with the Great Dirauj in the east- Stupid man... You are more Fu'Aitauz[1] than he ever could be," she says with a lump in her throat.

Mald nods and looks up at his mother. Everything that could be said to her about his father had already been said, but that doesn't stop him reminding her.

"We fought those wars for the same reasons we are having this marriage. To allow us to thrive. So that what happened in the past won't be repeated. So we won't be torn apart," he says simply.

His eyes find Jheal doing chore work for some of the other tribesmen.

"I want to raise Jheal and Sha to be 'Ifacho. Not some hostage-princes of the Dirauj. Not some Terkizcho. Not like I nor Tijjikauz," he says watching Jheal run.

Shiva responds. "This marriage shows our willingness to join hands with Tijjikauz and his master. This is true. But it also makes us equal to Tijjikauz in the eyes of the Great Dirauj. It is a dream to believe that Tijjikauz will allow us to choose any option other than theirs. Coalition leads the lesser to be subservient. And we are the lesser."

Behind Mald the tent flaps open again. He turns and he catches a glimpse of Talia and his daughters in the tent before it flaps back down.

---

1. Fu'Aitauz [fu.'.ait.auws] : Cavalry Leader, or Leader – lit. "fu'ait" horse, "-auz" equivalent to English -er, eg. Carpenter

"We are why he is where he is. We are equal... Are we done here mother?" says Mald changing the subject.

"Yes Fu'Aitauz," says Shiva, "I do believe we have what we need. The dowry. The supplies. And thanks to our merchant friends, even the spirits."

Shiva waves a hand behind her over the rest of the tribespeople as she mentally marks off her checklist.

Mald hadn't realised it but all of his people were already beginning to pack up.

"Tight leash ao'Shiva, as always," Mald replies quickly and with a smile.

His mother glares at him, looking for an insult in the honorific.

Mald wears an innocent look, but continues to smile at her.

"akal'Mald-," a thin voice calls out to the group.

Mald closes his left eye down hard, as if hearing a loud piercing noise.

A thin man surrounded by a few of the town's guards, all men clad in brown-grey coloured armour, approach the group. The thin man has silver speckled in his hair, but his walk belies his age, each step had the strength and purpose of a commander. To his left and right people stop to let him have his way.

Mald closes his eyes.

"I thought we could get away with not seeing him this trip. He only ever brings with him a storm," Mald grumbles to Shiva quietly before slowly turning towards the man.

He dips his head to the thin man in a greeting.

"akal'Shiv'Anu, may you find shade."

Shiv'Anu responds. "And may you find shade, old friend."

Shiv'Anu looks around the packing tribesmen. Raises an eyebrow and turns back to Mald.

"Leaving already?"

"No, no. Not quite yet. But our business is done here for now."

Around Mald his people continue to pack up. To the untrained observer they might have looked like they weren't clearly eavesdropping, but his warriors were watching. He could see them out of the corners of his eyes cautiously steeling themselves in case they are forced to fight and flee. In most places around the desert this would be the correct intuition, he couldn't deny that. It was something almost born into being an 'Ifacho.

He sighs.

The idea that he and Tijjikauz had, once upon a time, was that *here* would be different.

The market begins to hush, as if in anticipation.

Shiv'Anu's few armed men shuffle uncomfortably, unconsciously feeling the tension.

Mald can see his own people are getting more and more anxious and in turn making Shiv'Anu's guards anxious. A cycle that only increases as it repeats.

"The hourglass turns, akal," he says quietly.

Shiv'Anu nods.

Mald can tell that he can feel the tension too.

Shiv'Anu looks over his shoulder to who must be his second-in-command, a young man with fresh scars across his arms. He is tense, hand on his sword, but unlike his men who are nervously surveying the tribesmen he is staring straight at Mald.

Mald recognises the look in his eyes, even if he didn't recognise the man himself. It's a look that can start wars.

"Come akal. Let us talk in private," says Mald trying to cut the tension and move away from this young man's hawkish stare. With that he waves a hand towards his tent.

Shiv'Anu nods and looks back to his men.

"That suits me fine, 'Ifacho," he says while using his hand to wave down his guards, their hands on their swords. The casual use of the word 'Ifacho cause his city guards to relax. Only someone who knows he is safe would dare call the tribesmen that.

The guards relax, but only a little.

The second-in-command, however, doesn't back down.

"Release," says Shiv'Anu quietly. His command is not to be disobeyed.

The second-in-command relaxes after a split-second.

Mald gives the slightest of nods at the second-in-command, but never breaks eye contact with Shiv'Anu.

After another moment the second-in-command then raises his hand. The other guards understand the command to stay where they are.

Odd. They seem to respond to that second-in-command more readily than Shiv'Anu.

Mald turns and makes eye contact with his warriors.

They nod in response. His command is also understood and obeyed, they won't move unless it's necessary.

Mald turns back to Shiv'Anu with a smile and leads him towards his tent. Lifting the bottom flaps up Mald enters first, with Shiv'Anu following right behind him.

Talia and the girls are within the tent.

"My shivauz. Has a'Sha been found yet-". Talia stops short when she sees the guard commander behind her husband. An unreadable expression crosses her face as she looks from him to Mald.

Mald walks to the middle of the tent and stops.

With a slow hiss he draws his sword.

Slowly he turns on Shiv'Anu wearing a serious expression.

Shiv'Anu doesn't react immediately, he merely raises an eyebrow in response.

Tension amplifies the sounds of the outside world.

With a sigh Talia rolls her eyes and gets to her feet with a slight groan.

"akal'Shiv'Anu," says Talia speaking around her husband. She bows her head in respect as she speaks. Her hands behind her, she signals to her daughters to do the same.

The children awkwardly copy the bow.

Shiv'Anu accepts their respectful gestures with grace.

"Come girls," Talia says turning to her girls after they bow and leading them out.

As the girls pass they each in turn bow a second time and mutter "akal."

Shiv'Anu nods to each, even to the little one, who cracks him a cheeky smile.

The brown tent flap swishes along the ground, leaving the two men alone.

Mald, sword still in hand, lets out a loud laugh.

"a'Anu," Mald shakes his head, "even after all the stories you still don't fear my madness?"

With a smooth motion Mald sticks his sword into the ground between them, a sign of disarmament and trust. He takes his hand off of his sword and puts his hands on his hips with a large grin across his face.

Shiv'Anu shakes his head.

"Just because it has been a long time since we were in the desert together doesn't mean I've forgotten the old ways. Also if you do it every time, someday someone is going to react-."

Subtly, however, Mald can see that Shiv'Anu relaxes. Mirroring Mald, he draws his sword and sticks it into the ground across Mald's own.

"-And the stories of 'Ifacho madness serve their purpose, but I was there when they were created... and I know their truth."

They embrace like the old friends they are and pull away after a few moments and a few thuds on each other's backs.

"My old friend-" Mald says as he takes a seat on his ruby-coloured floor mat next to a large circular bronze table, "-what brings you here on this day? I wasn't expecting to see you until the wedding?"

On top of the bronze table is a large blue-and-white ceramic teapot with a couple matching mugs on either side. He offers Shiv-'Anu a seat with a wave to the other floor mat.

Shiv'Anu takes him up on his offer and lowers himself less than gracefully with his mail armour clanging around him.

"If you want one of my white horses," Mald says "it'll cost you more than a guard commander's, or a governor's for that matter, salary... Tea?"

Shiv'Anu shakes his head.

"Too sweet," he says.

"Right. Right. I forgot. Poison from the east."

Shiv'Anu frowns. With a shrug Mald pours one for himself and, after a thought, one for Shiv'Anu regardless of his objections.

"Speaking of my silvers... It is with great regret I must inform you that they will cost more now," Mald remarks conversationally.

"More than a kingdom?"

"More than an empire. Especially after the other night."

Mald looks at his old friend.

Shiv'Anu is gazing, seemingly idly, around the tent until his eyes linger on something. Mald can't quite read his expression so he follows Shiv'Anu's eyes to a small delicate tapestry. It shows a walled city being sieged by horsemen.

They both stare.

The tapestry is a dedication to a time they both knew in their youth.

Mald breaks the silence.

"What brings you here today a'Anu?"

Shiv'Anu responds quickly.

"How could I not come and inspect when a violent, infamous 'Ifacho comes into the city that I have charge of."

Mald snorts.

Shiv'Anu speaks more slowly now.

"You spoke of the other night... It's curious you know, incidents have happened recently here also. Some-".

His eyes sharply cross to meet Mald's.

"-'Ifacho raided *my* southern merchants."

Shiv'Anu spreads his arms.

"Nothing too serious. It seems our gold was secondary to their interests. Of course they took some, but left too much."

Shiv'Anu looks around the tent. The impression of a desert owl searching for a vole is strong.

"But the wares, leather, bronze, weapons…" Shiv'Anu looks at Mald's blue silk clothes. "The ocean silk you sold us. *That* they all took. I do hope that they were not friends of yours. If so I should tell you that the ones we found had their tongues taken and were forced to take the walk."

Shiv'Anu and Mald hold their gaze.

Mald ever so slightly shakes his head.

The guard commander then shifts his view to look at the tent flaps, almost as if trying to peer out of the tent itself, before changing the subject.

"I must admit that I do want one of your horses… If you want to give in to your better nature and give one to me. As a replacement to the one I had in my youth. Or even as a way to smooth over the 'Ifacho raid that occurred."

"You flatter me, a'Anu, thinking I have a better nature. I am no noble, no Dirauj. I am merely a wanderer of the sands, an 'Ifacho. You know how we are. As you were once." Mald says with an unreadable smile. "In our youth you never struck me as one to leave the ocean of sand and settle."

Shiv'Anu's silence gives the impression that ice could form in the corners of the tent.

"-And all the way up to governor and guard commander no less…"

Mald takes a slow sip of his tea before continuing.

"To tell the truth, I was… surprised… to hear that Tijjikauz granted you the Governorship also."

The silence holds.

Beneath Mald's words both men understand the implication, "but I was more surprised that you accepted to… settle."

Breaking the tension Mald laughs and smiles a tooth grin.

"Regardless. No. I will not give you one for free. And as I was not involved nor had any knowledge of that raid, blood money is not a requirement. I will however promise to look into it, if that can settle you. Though you might get a discount if you come back to the sand."

Shiv'Anu brushes off the denial.

"Well," he says, "no large matter. I *will* have one of those horses one day-".

He then looks at Mald.

"-and I will breed them. And then supply them to my men here in the guard. And who knows maybe even the Great Dirauj will buy them from me and make me a lesser Dirauj, lesser than Tijjikauz of course."

Mald gives Shiv'Anu a suspicious but good-natured glance.

Shiv'Anu sighs and takes on a more serious tone.

"I've found that sometimes we must do what we don't expect or want..."

Shiv'Anu lets the silence linger again as he thinks about what to say next.

"My Friend, you know I am not here to merely chat."

Mald sighs and glances down at his scarred and boney knuckles. When did his hands get so old. On his fingers sat three rings. Until now he had been playing with a brilliant sapphire set into one of them. He stops himself. If he kept playing any more the gem could come undone.

With a slow but steady movement of his head he looks up at the man who he once considered a spear-brother.

"He is already getting my daughter. He has my support, and with that support he even has the ocean of sand... or at least, peace within it. We have turned a blind eye to his political manoeuvring, and been his spear and shield. But here we can't unsee the fodder being picked up. They are not warriors. These are not honourable men."

Shiv'Anu snorts at the word 'honourable'.

Mald intentionally ignores him as he continues.

"Most do not seem like warriors, or even men, at all. These are the shadows of men. And I am not so blind as to not see what is being prepared. I hate those ships. Only the foolish would allow them to be so close. That warfare goes against what it means to be a man."

Mald's words hang in the air.

"With all respect due that is due, akal'Mald," says Shiv'Anu without malice in his voice. "You are bonded to the Dirauj and his will to war. It is your duty-"

"a'Anu, please. Once, a lifetime ago, we fought together. We fought with and against those Terkizcho. But that ship. I remember ships like those. I remember the sickness of those shadow men-"

Mald unconsciously shakes his head and shudders.

"-and these- these *warriors*."

He almost spits at the word.

"Fodder. Tell me honestly. Will he use those dead ships as his weapon as they were once used against us?"

Shiv'Anu looks Mald dead in his dark eyes.

Silence.

"Every man has a master," Shiv'Anu says. "Even 'Ifacho. Even Tijjikauz. Even me. Especially me. But your pledge of support to the Dirauj means answering his call, whenever akal'Tijjikauz calls. Without questioning who holds his leash as he holds yours."

"We will not be fodder," Mald replies without emotion.

Both men stare at each other.

Both men wait.

As if the outside world releases its breath sound flows back around the tent.

Shiv'Anu is the first to speak.

"Another war is coming. More than just in the south. The lions are waking up. Join together, like akal'Kali before you... or fight everyone. Alone."

"Is that a threat, old friend?"

Shiv'Anu sighs and gets to his feet.

"Not a threat. Advice."

Suddenly the tent flap behind Shiv'Anu opens up.

Shiv'Anu spins, instinctively reaching out to his sword. He relaxes as he sees that it is one of his own guards.

"Sir, we-".

Almost knocking him over comes Ilatr.

"akal'Mald! ao'Jalila and a'Sha have been hurt."

Mald looks from Ilatr to Shiv'Anu, who nods.

Shiv'Anu withdraws his sword from the ground and sheaths it by his side.

Mald moves quickly and with a soft hiss his sword finds its home in the sheath by his side.

"We will continue this later akal'Shiv'Anu," he says and walks out of the tent without a look back.

MALD

THE MARKETPLACE IS IN CHAOS. In front of his tent a whirlwind of his people seem to be blocking off the local city folk and town guards. A wooden table is overthrown at the leftmost edge of his sight. He turns to see one of his people has been pushed over it. Thankfully he catches his tribesman's eye before he can draw his knife.

"Control and do not engage." Mald tells Ilatr.

Ilatr nods and moves towards the crowd to calm his people.

Mald needs to get control before this all turns to bloodshed.

From all corners come echoing shouts, threats and commands. Mald can hardly see through the throng and can hardly hear anything through the cacophony. He forces his way through to the centre of it all and comes out to a small clearing.

Mald's tribe are all in an uproar, all grouped around a bleeding a'Sha and a blood-covered and injured Jalila kneeling over him.

Shiv'Anu's guards have taken a step back, in an effort to pull onlookers away from the angry crowd. Town guards they may be, but they will not move or take more action than necessary unless they are given an order.

Mald has seen mobs like this before. All it takes is one of the city folk to push one of his tribe to create a riot. He takes immediate charge of his people.

"Get a'Sha into the tent."

His people take a second to respond to his command.

"Now."

The word and his will have power. They take notice.

He directs the tribesmen with his hands to take them into the tent he just came out of. As one, his people who are closest to a'Sha close around him and pick him up delicately to carry him into Mald's tent.

Jalila tries to follow but is forced back down to her knees by the pain and loss of blood.

She has lost too much blood.

Movement from out of the corner of his eye causes him to turn.

He spots Talia and his girls watching the scene. Talia is covering her youngest's eyes, but a'Diwa has her mouth open in disgust and shock.

To their left he sees his own mother and Jheal. Jheal is in tears. Shiva has her arms around him. She is trying to turn him away but he won't budge.

Mald gestures at her and grabs her attention.

"Take Jheal and my girls away, Mother. They do not need to see this."

His mother takes a moment to respond but nods and drags the family away.

Mald watches them enter a barren tent. The inside is almost completely packed.

His tribesmen weren't completely ready to leave yet, but they needed to be now. With a look around he signals for the rest to leave more quickly.

He turns and kneels down by Jalila to inspect how hurt she is.

a'Sha's belt scarf is wrapped haphazardly around her right eye. He leaves it tied. Taking it off here could be much worse.

Then he looks down and inspects the deep cut across her chest.

She is losing a lot of blood. That needs to be attended to as soon as possible.

But first.

He takes a deep breath and asks with a soft but firm voice.

"What happened?"

Jalila responds quickly but quietly between gasps of pain.

"It's a dead ship Mald. A Black ship. Everyone was dead. I was right. I was-".

The world seems to come into sharp focus as Mald understands what Jalila is saying. He looks up from her with a wild fury burning his eyes, as goosebumps line his arms, and a feeling of disgust shivers through him. He finds his target and points at Shiv'Anu.

"I could not- *would* not believe that was a Black Ship when I saw it. Even if I had guessed it to be so. No one could be so foolish to keep one so close to the shore, but you let it be docked here!"

Mald shakes as he speaks. He is breathing heavily.

Jalila puts her hand on his and tries to calm him, but he can't hear her. He is tunnel visioned on Shiv'Anu.

Incomprehension blankets Shiv'Anu's face, then anger twists it.

He turns to one of his guards and says something Mald can't make out.

Mald feels Jalila's hand squeeze his harder.

He looks down at her.

Jalila speaks between breaths.

"a'Sha snuck onto the ship. He was caught-, but we got away. We have to leave."

Jalila looks pleading and demanding at the same time.

Mald looks into her one visible eye. She may be in pain but her judgement isn't clouded.

He realises his own is.

"We need to leave Mald," she repeats. "Now."

Mald nods, head cleared, and turns to Shiv'Anu.

Shiv'Anu has already begun moving, not in fear of the tribesmen's wrath, but in preparation. He shouts out an angry command at his second-in-command, who merely nods and signals his own command to the other guards. They scatter in a controlled manner.

Shiv'Anu turns back to find Mald looking at him. Contrary to the previous angry outburst Mald has calmed himself, but there is a certain glint in his eye that makes the hair on the back of Shiv'Anu's neck stand on edge.

"My friend, we shall continue our discussion later–" Shiv'Anu begins, but gets cut off by Mald.

"I never for a second thought you would be involved with those ships Shiv'Anu. Not again. Not truly. Let alone be foolish enough to let it dock."

There are no pleasantries in his speech, no acknowledgement of rank or closeness.

Shiv'Anu looks down for a moment, but remembering who he is and his rank quickly stares right back at Mald. Expression fades from his face.

Shiv'Anu takes a deep breath before responding.

"You should know, akal'Tijjikauz will expect you to answer his call." Shiv'Anu lowers his voice now so that only Mald and Jalila can hear him in the chaos. "I have a feeling my 'Ifacho problem and the horse raid on your camp–"

Mald is slightly taken aback, but doesn't let it show.

How did he know? Mald was sure he didn't mention about the horse raid.

Shiv'Anu continues.

"The world turns even when you aren't, my friend. You weren't that far from my walls. I think our problems are related. But my hands are tied. If I were you, I would leave Kiraj. Now. Before the sand settles."

With that Shiv'Anu lets out another bark of a command and moves off in the direction of the port before Mald can respond.

"Remember what I told you Fu'Aitauz," Shiv'Anu calls out behind his back. "Don't turn your back on us."

The Hourglass That Swallows You

Shiv'Anu disappears into the crowd, guardsmen following closely behind.

A deep loud breath from Jalila next to him returns him to the now.

Mald's voice cuts through the chaos.

"We need to leave. Now. Ilatr!"

From the crowd comes his lithe second-in-command.

"When she is in the tent, go help Mother. Tell her we must leave."

"Of course," Ilatr replies.

Then he helps Jalila into the barren tent.

An island in the flow of movement Mald looks around at his rushing tribe and closes his eyes, listening to the pounding of feet and boots on dirt and stone and sand.

It's all too much. Too much, too fast and with no time to think.

With a jolt his eyes open. His father's words echo in the distance of his brain.

Just move your feet and body and mind will follow.

He looks around and finds everyone is doing what he told them, then turns and follows his family into his tent.

JALILA

It takes Jalila's eyes minutes to adjust to the dusty gloom of Mald's tent. Agonising, extra-temporal minutes pass by that seem to last forever, but as surely as the hourglass turns do they pass.

Yet what she sees can't be real.

This all can't be real.

How has everything changed so quickly, and so drastically.

Her a'Sha was playing but a moment ago.

He can't be dying.

Jalila is kneeling on the ground, knees on the floor and staring down at her son with her one good eye. A position that once upon a time the zealots of the Western Eye Church would force her to adopt to feel the light of the all-father. The light has long since disappeared, all she can feel now are the tears rolling down her cheeks.

Her arms burn from fatigue but she can't stop putting as much pressure on the cut on a'Sha's neck as feels safe.

Her eye begins to sting and she brings up a damp, warm hand to wipe it away. It leaves a trail of her son's blood over her forehead. Without even noticing the blood on her hands, she brings her hand back down to continue applying pressure onto her son's neck.

She is uncomfortable, unable to keep still or control her breathing. The rhythm of her heart feels the same as a horses gallop. Her lungs don't seem to be able to hold any breath.

a'Sha's belt-scarf feels loose around her head. She tries to tighten it but doing so forces her to take her hand off of her son.

She chooses to let the belt-scarf fall instead, exposing her wound to the sharp musty air.

"You're okay," she mutters at her a'Sha under her breath over and over and over.

Next to her is a bucket of rose-coloured water. She decides to lift the scarf she has around a'Sha's neck, thankfully the bleeding has slowed.

Her panic subsides a bit.

There would be *a lot more* blood if it had cut too deep.

Thank the shadel.

But it must be cleaned. That ship was filth, those weapons were sickness. She has to clean him.

She places the scarf on her lap and continues her cleaning, but she is struggling against her own fatigue. She drops the dirty scarf into the water and twists her body to pick up a new rag. She twists a bit too much and quietly yelps in pain at the deep cut across her chest.

She grits her teeth. Her eye is pulsing in pain.

a'Sha is ashen, but still breathing. His eyes are closed, but with every tap of the wet cloth comes an unconscious wince of pain.

"How is he?"

Jalila jumps at the sound of her brother's deep growl of a voice. She spins and sees Mald.

The fear gone she breathes out a sigh and pulls all of her focus back to her son.

Mald kneels down beside her.

"He's hurt, a'Ma. My little crown, he- he is really hurt."

She pulls the rag off again as before. Another whimper.

"He has lost so much blood," she says simply.

"As have you."

She feels his hand softly take the rag over, "let me help-".

He tries to take over from her but she resists.

He sighs and lets go.

"Let me at least try to address your wounds."

Jalila cuts him off sharply. "I'm fine," she says, "just focus on him."

Behind her she hears a sharp intake of air. She turns to see her brother moving away from her.

He is staring at the bite wound around her leg with eyes wide.

The bloody bite mark is oozing a liquid the colour of sand.

"a'Jali that is not okay," he says unable to hide the involuntary panic and disgust in his voice. "That gash-".

She cuts him off.

"It's nothing. I'm fine. Caught my leg on the wood," she snaps, downplaying the lie, her voice breaking. "Please- please. Just help my son."

Mald, with some difficulty, moves closer to them both. He sits beside her and reaches over to pick up a clean rag. Gingerly he passes it to her, trying to avoid her leg as much as possible.

They work in silence.

Jalila can feel people come in and go behind her but ignores them, they are blurs to the sharp reality of her son's condition.

After a time Mald moves away and she can hear him talking in hushed tones behind her.

"I should have been there faster," she says under her breath, "I should have. I'm so sorry. It's all my fault."

"It's not your fault," says Mald softly moving back into position to help her. "But what happens to all of us next could depend on what you tell me now."

Jalila delicately dabs at her son.

"I was furious. I was ready to leave him out for the shadel and he knew it. So he ran. He was so fast. I couldn't catch him. I should have-".

She grasps her hands together and closes her good eye.

"I heard him scream at the dock. He screamed from that death ship. And my entire world fell."

Mald's only response is to clench his jaw.

"The ship was dead," she says softly. "Everywhere was sickness. Everywhere was death."

She takes a deep breath before continuing.

Her glare screams fire.

"You said they never docked. You said they would *never* dock... *Never* Mald. Except at war. And I don't think we are at war."

She peers into the dark of Mald's eyes and a shiver of realisation runs down her spine. She can see the pain of remembrance there, nevertheless the words hang.

"Are we going to war?"

He doesn't answer but she can see his mind turn the hourglass and watch the dust settle.

Her son lets out a low whimper.

She turns back to him. He is shivering despite the heat and there is nothing she can do. So she continues to dab.

"We can't stay here," she says.

"We are leaving as soon as everyone is ready," Mald says through the storm in his head. "It's too fast... Everything is moving too fast. You must be wrong."

"I am not wrong Mald. That ship was exactly as you described," Jalila says exasperated.

"Enough!" Mald snaps at her. "Enough. I still can't believe it. Not even after both you and Shiv'Anu have confirmed it. We need to move to keep ahead. We will keep everyone safe a'Jali."

Mald gets to his feet, discussion over.

"We- I need to make sure everyone is ready to go."

Mald turns to leave.

Jalila glares at her brother's back.

"I..." she hesitates, "I... I killed an officer on that ship."

Mald stops, his back to her. She can't see his face.

Silence.

Mald doesn't turn.

"The Dirauj will not react well to this..." he says in a level tone. "But what is done, is done. You did what you had to."

The tent flap opens suddenly to reveal Ilatr, silhouetted by the yellowed light outside. In his hands is a rough stretcher.

Jalila stares at him briefly. Eyes blinded by the shift in light around them.

Then she looks around to find the tent is almost completely empty. She hadn't noticed.

"akal'Mald, ao'Jalila," says Ilatr. "Everyone else is ready to go. ao'Talia and a'Diwa are just outside. We need to move a'Sha and leave."

Mald nods and moves towards his second-in-command, who moves aside.

At the threshold he pauses.

"Was he bitten?" Mald asks.

Jalila doesn't respond, instead she simply stares at her son.

The tent and the wind seem to hold their breath.

"I don't think so," she says after an endless moment, "but- I don't know."

"We will know in less than seven days," he says. "Before the ceremony even. Prepare for the choice we might have to make."

Mald then grabs the other end of the rough stretcher.

He and Ilatr quickly but delicately place a'Sha onto the stretcher and move the boy outside to their transport. The transport is made up of a camel carting a small bed underneath a small brown canopy.

Jalila hasn't moved.

"I had to- He was going to kill a'Sha-" Jalila begins.

Mald finally turns to look at his sister.

"As long as he wasn't bitten," he says, "We will figure this out, but you *must* heal. And we *must* get back to the Oasis as quickly as possible."

Then he leaves.

Pain suddenly washes over her. All of her focus was on her son but now that he is out of her sight her body feels heavy. She tries to stand and follow the men, but her head becomes cloudy. She can feel the darkness tunnelling her vision.

Wind rushes past her ears as she tumbles backwards.

Talia and Diwa are there before she falls.

They set Jalila back down gently. They are talking to her but she can't focus on the words. They sound distant, somehow thunderous but blurry at the same time. Jalila's head swivels drunkenly down to her leg.

It's still bleeding. Slowly, but surely.

As if by magic a bandage appears around it.

Diwa is tightening it and looking at her. Even through the haze Jalila can make out that her eyes are red and puffy. She tries to embrace the girl but can't lift her arms high enough.

All around the tent blurs come and pack the remnants of it.

Jalila feels a tight squeeze around her leg and looks down as Diwa finishes tightening the bandage.

Gently all three of them stand with Jalila between them and hobble slowly into the heat and sun.

Behind the tribespeople collapse the tent.

DIWA

WHILST THEY WERE NOT AS FAST as their silvery-white horses, the tribespeople's camels travelled with incredible momentum and consistency.

The stone houses of Kiraj'it'Jalila all blend together around Diwa as she walks beside her tribe's camel train.

The 'Ifacho were beating a hasty retreat out of the city.

Not the first time they had ever had to beat a hasty retreat from a city.

They, the people from the cities, just never seemed to welcome her or her family. She couldn't understand it.

Yet despite that, all she could think of right now was jumping off the camel and running back into the city. It didn't matter how or where. She just wanted to go.

Some drunken townspeople stare as they go but most are too focused on their alcohol and the celebrations, ignoring the 'Ifacho by intentionally avoiding their gaze. It seems that news of the commotion in the market square had been slowed by the festivities.

Diwa's cheeks burned as she tried to stare out over the quickly evaporating city. She hadn't been slapped physically but ao'Shiva's tongue-lashing had left its mark nonetheless.

She opens her mouth to speak a defence but finds no words come out. Instead she continues to stare at the ground and walk forward beside the camel train.

ao'Shiva towered above her on a camel like some sort of lesser dirauj.

"Shadel willing," ao'Shiva says shaking her head and continuing with her tirade, "we will be back in the Oasis and you *will* be ready in time. And I will not hear another word of argument."

Diwa couldn't look at her. Instead the smell of the sea air causes Diwa to look to her left and out in the direction of the azure sea, which she could just make out through the derelict old city.

They have made it to the outskirts of the ruined city with surprising haste.

Diwa sighs.

She was promised that she would be able to explore a bit.

Maybe even go into the sea…

She loved the sea. Memories of running and jumping into it with her mother and aunt flicker through her head. That was all she ever wanted to do. Jump in the water every day. But it was a rare treat. Now because of her brother and cousin she wouldn't be able to do it again for some time.

If ever.

Must and the dust of the desert reverses the smell of the sea, and brings her out of her daydreaming. She idly sucks her teeth and wrinkles her nose. The smell of the desert, of heat and dirt, was overwhelming.

Stifling. It was always there, like a shadel trying to pull her into the sand.

There was tension in the air, and she could feel it. She could even hear it in ao'Shiva's shrill more-strained-than-usual voice.

Her little sister Kita's voice catches her attention. Her eyes swivel to where she is.

She is trying to play with Jheal, but Jheal isn't biting.

Diwa, under her breath, says, "he didn't get into much trouble, did he?"

She looks back to the sea and sighs again, she has cried enough. The momentary escape that was promised to her had been taken.

Now the mature thing to do was to turn back to the future. The wedding has been set in stone since at least the last Festival of 'Ifa Shadelna, seven turns ago. She could still remember when they told her about it a couple of turns later, though the memories themselves were fuzzy.

She was only a few turns younger than her brother then.

And "the Bastard".

No.

That last thought causes her to shake her head, angry at herself. She had promised herself she would stop calling him that, at least out in public.

Shaking her head loosens her head scarf. Exposing her head to the unyielding sun.

As she tightens it again the words of her mother come back to her.

Take care of how you think, and you will change how you act.

Truth be told she was worried about Sha. He looked like he was hurt. Truly hurt.

"Do you have the knife?" ao'Shiva asks.

Apparently she was still talking at her.

Diwa hadn't heard a word.

"I'm sorry Shi- I mean ao'Shiva. Yes."

Diwa puts her hand down to her side and taps a short ivory handled dagger.

"Good. Keep it safe, you will need to give it to akal'Tijjikauz during the ceremony. It symbolises a surrendering of defence to-" ao'Shiva continues, but Diwa tunes her out again.

She looks back out to the sea.

She had heard all of this before at least a few dozen times. But the sea was ever changing, or so her father said. She would like that. Some change from this dusty, barren ocean of sand.

She finds her eyes and her attention falls back to her cousin, Sha.

She had only caught a glimpse of him back in Kiraj'it'Jalila after the... *event*.

She spots the covered camel transport that he is in. That transport was for anyone who needed the shade during long journeys.

She sighed.

I need the shade too. But that idiot had to go and get himself hurt.

Again she shook her head.

You aren't being fair, she chides herself, the injured need that shade more and there is no doubt that *he* is hurt.

Still.

Walking beside the transport she spots her mother beside Jalila. Everyone said her mother was the voice of reason behind her father and ao'Shiva. Even mother couldn't argue me out of this.

Father always gets his way.

Jalila slumps forward a little, as if she were about to pass out.

Ilatr rushes forward to catch her.

Diwa feels her heart skip a beat, and her face goes red despite the sun and the forgotten argument.

Had he always been there?

How could she have not noticed?

She continues to stare at Ilatr as he abruptly stops trying to help Jalila.

She is so strong, but so stubborn. Diwa could remember her father saying that Jalila and Shiva were like two stones. Strong, hard and unbending, but completely unable to interact without grinding each other down.

Diwa's feet move before her mind tells them not to and she walks over to the group around the transport.

Another breeze blows in from the sea. The salt in the air is lesser now that they are further outside the city, but she could still catch a hint of it. She felt as if she would follow it anywhere it took her.

Behind her, somewhere in the mists of her recognition, she could still hear ao'Shiva's voice chatting to her.

She ignored it.

For her part ao'Shiva hadn't yet noticed that Diwa was walking away anyway.

A large gold and ruby necklace catches the sun on Ilatr's defined, deep golden chest, glinting like fire into her eyes.

She loved that unusual necklace. She had asked him about it once. It was a dowry gift from someone in the East long ago, while he and her father were caught in that war.

Diwa recalled the moment he spoke to her about it.

She blushed despite herself.

The memory was still as vivid as the campfire reflecting in his eyes had been. He told her about the Eastern family who gave it to him. The story was of bravery and heroism. He was a warrior in blue and on a pure white horse who saved a king and was rewarded a daughter as a gift...

The ending of the thought brought her back to her reality and she felt as if she was going to throw up.

Am I to be just some gift?

How could this be the way of the world?

Why was this *her* duty?

Why couldn't she just run like her aunt had done?

The other women in the tribe had said that this was just the shadel whispering doubts into her ears. That she should never trust the shadel. That it is a beautiful thing to be wed, doubly so to such a great warrior. But she couldn't get the feeling that it was all wrong out of her head.

She can feel the tears welling up inside her again.

Ahead she could see her aunt and mother, but not Ilatr.

While she was lost in her memories Ilatr must have left.

Too late to turn around now she continues her pace towards the women.

At least with them she could claim ignorance to ao'Shiva.

Within a couple of paces she catches up.

The swelling across auntie's eye was growing larger. The bandage was a dark red and dull yellow… and loose.

I'll need to retie it, she thought to herself.

Within the transport beside her aunt, Sha stirs.

Jalila turns to check on him, loosening the eye bandage further. The movement causes Godshome and the Sun to shine in their conjoined multi-coloured way towards Diwa. She turns so as to not let herself be blinded.

They have reached the furthest outskirts of the city now, but the tower by the sea that lends Kiraj'it'Jalila its name can still be seen, like a watchmen over the wine-dark sea. At this time of dusk it was beautiful, wrapped as if by a cloak like some sort of dirauj in the golden, red and purple glow of the dusk.

"I'll come back," Diwa says to herself under her breath.

She turns back around to the women sharply.

Jalila is deep in thought while staring at the transport.

She winces in pain suddenly and reaches down to what is causing it. The bandage she has wrapped around her leg is oozing red and yellow.

Diwa glances at the other gashes as she walks over to them. They don't look as if they are still bleeding. Except for the one on Jalila's leg.

Jalila peels back the bandage around her leg slowly. It looks excruciating. She shudders with pain at the open and angry wound. She stares at it for a few moments. Then, almost as if trying to hide a gift, she delicately reties the bandage.

To Diwa it feels like she is catching a glimpse of something she shouldn't be. Unconsciously she strains her neck to try not to look away. She sees Jalila straighten back up. At the same time Jalila's eyes go fuzzy, as if she sat up too fast.

She slumps over and forward using the nearest camel as support.

Diwa rushes forward towards her.

"Auntie?"

Jalila turns to see her looking concerned. Her mind seems to uncloud. She flashes a quick pained smile and then looks at Sha beside her.

"It just hurts a little... Don't worry too much. Thank you a'Diwa."

Diwa tries to smile back at her but her eyes are still glassy from crying before. She looks at Sha and then back to her aunt.

"I'm sure he will be alright, Auntie. He's too annoying to stay down for long," Diwa says while extending a hand to holds Jalila's.

Jalila nods while they hold hands for a brief moment.

"I- I'm sorry I snapped at you earlier," says Diwa. "Before all... Of this... It was wrong of me. I shouldn't have been so rude. You were only trying to help."

"Don't worry about that," Jalila says with that same smile. Her voice is strained, as if trying to hold her breath and grit her teeth at the same time.

"Auntie are-" Diwa begins but Jalila cuts her off.

"-Is your brother holding up alright?"

Diwa looks forward.

"Seems fine... But I can tell he is worried about Sha too. He has less... fire I guess. He isn't as loud-".

Diwa pauses as she recalls the whirlwind of events of the past couple of days.

"And that's saying something," she continues. "I think it's been ever since the attack a few nights ago. When he protected us against that thug."

Jalila sighs and looks at her with her one good eye.

"What he did was something that had to be done," she says, "but it is never easy. It never should be."

Diwa can clearly see the cogs turning.

Jalila takes a moment before speaking.

"You are *all* so grown up already. But it's too soon for all of you," she says, her voice breaking.

She rubs her eye, then continues, "I wish I could have changed all of this. I'm so sorry, a'Diwa."

"Auntie, what are you talking about?" Diwa says while she moves to give her a hug. "a'Sha and a'Jheal running off wasn't your fault. They are stupid kids."

Jalila gives a little hollow chuckle and embraces the hug.

"You are so mature already, a'Diwa."

She then pulls away to look at her niece...

Diwa's cheeks turn crimson, but an unsure smile spreads across her expression.

"And yet... soon you won't be my a'Diwa anymore, you'll be ao'Diwa to us."

"I'll always be a'Diwa for you."

Shiva's shrill command cuts through the air.

"a'Diwa? a'Diwa get back here. Where did you run off too now."

Much like her father Diwa closes one eye down at the sound of someone's voice that she doesn't want to hear.

"Oh fun," Diwa responds under her breath to Jalila as she sneaks a peak in the direction of ao'Shiva, who is looking around for her.

"I can't wait for the day to become ao'Diwa for *her*."

Diwa turns back to Jalila who is smiling broadly.

"Good luck with that."

They both laugh together.

"But you'll find she isn't so bad really. She loves you more than you could ever realise. You'll understand it more when you have a child yourself."

The thought isn't allowed to settle as Shiva continues.

"There you are a'Diwa. Stop bothering the injured and get over here."

ao'Shiva's voice echoes over the tribespeople.

More than a few of them unconsciously cower.

Diwa takes a last long look at Sha through the semi-transparent transport sheeting and sees the blood-red bandage around his neck. Even if it is just some sort of trick of the light or the shadel fooling her, he looks like he has some of his colour back.

Then Diwa trudges, her shoulders hunched, towards her grandmother's voice.

She glances back at Jalila helplessly.

Jalila laughs and raises her shoulders.

No help there.

With the grace of the final drop of sand the sun finally falls over the crest of the dunes.

JALILA

IT IS past noon in the desert a day later. The camel train is still on its way back into the depths of the ocean of sand, towards their latest place to call home. The women are riding close together towards the back of the group near the transport.

The air is still and the heat intense.

Under the red and brown cover of the transport a'Sha lays in a troubled sleep, tossing and turning. He looks feverish. Each breath he takes leaves a crackle hanging in the air. Jalila is dabbing a'Sha's forehead with a damp cloth.

She leaves the cloth on his forehead and inspects the tightened scarf around his neck. It doesn't look like it's bleeding anymore, but she couldn't be sure.

Beside her, helping her, is Diwa.

On the other side of a'Sha is her mother, Shiva.

Feeling eyes upon her, Jalila looks up.

Diwa quickly looks away, but Shiva is clearly staring at the bandages on Jalila.

Jalila ignores her, but can't stop herself unconsciously raising her hand to the bandage around her head.

The pain doesn't matter.

Only a'Sha.

"Shadel help him," says Shiva out loud and to no one in particular.

Jalila passes Diwa the dirty cloth from a'Sha's forehead, who in return gives her a fresh new one.

Jalila dabs a'Sha's head with the fresh wet cloth.

"I can't tell if he is getting worse Mother."

Diwa looks at Jalila, but catches her grandmother's eye. Shiva's expression is unreadable.

The sound of people approaching grabs Jalila's attention. Talia and Kita draw up close to the transport. Jheal follows behind them, fidgeting with his robes and looking towards the ground.

"a'Jhea wanted to see how a'Sha is doing," says Talia.

Talia turns to pull Jheal closer to the transport.

Before Jalila can respond a'Kita pipes up.

"When will he start riding again auntie? When will he play with me again?"

Talia shushes her softly, but leaves the question in the air.

Jheal moves forward to see his cousin more clearly but doesn't say anything.

He quickly recoils with a sharp intake of air.

"Jheal don't be scared-" Jalila says as a sudden wave of dizziness washes over her. Her face turns pale as she struggles to have any words, any air, come out. Her hand unconsciously comes up to her covered eye.

It takes her a moment to get her breath back.

"Auntie? Why are your lips blue?" a'Kita's little voice sounds like a distant west-eye forest bird humming sweetly.

The world blurs as the edges of her vision grow darker.

Like a body without its shadel she turns to a'Kita, the distant bird, and softly says, "He will be up again soon, a'Ki." Then she turns back to Jheal, "but he needs rest."

Braver now Jheal moves closer to a'Sha. He reaches out a little arm to the bandage around a'Sha's neck, but stops short. He looks up at Jalila for permission.

"Softly," Jalila says.

Jheal softly touches his hand to a'Sha neck.

He recoils his hand quickly, a'Sha's slightly wet blood on his finger tips.

"The cut is deep," says Shiva switching her gaze from Jalila to Jheal, "come, a'Jhe, let's get away and leave him be."

Jheal nods his head, and turns to leave with Shiva's arm around his shoulder.

Talia holds a'Kita's hand and also leads her away. a'Kita throws a concerned glance over her shoulder to Jalila as she leaves, but says nothing.

Thinking herself alone with her son Jalila lets out the cough she had been holding in. It's a heavy raspy cough, deep from her belly.

She feels her leather water jug tap her side. Without looking she takes a deep swig from it.

She lets out a deep broken breath and notices Diwa looking at her concerned. She must have hung back.

"You can go a'Diwa," says Jalila, "I shall be fine here with him for the time being."

Diwa hesitates, looking for more than just a verbal confirmation before leaving.

Jalila nods with a strained smile.

Diwa clutches the sides of her robes and releases them. Clearly she wants to say something, but she isn't sure enough of herself or the thought. Instead she turns without saying anything and trails the rest of the women leaving Jalila finally alone with her son.

Jalila stares at her only child.

Another wave of dizziness washes over her and her feet feel unsteady, as if the wound had turned her leg to metal. She loses her balance and begins to tumble sideways.

Rough hands catch her shoulders.

"Hey. ao'Jalila?"

Dizzy Jalila looks up at the glowing outline of Ilatr.

"I'm- I'll- It's okay," she manages to get out. With force of will she gently pushes herself out of Ilatr's arms. She rubs her good but bloodshot eye and wraps the cloak around herself tighter. The cut across her chest causes her to grit her teeth but she bears the pain with a deep steadying breath.

Ilatr smiles at her. His pose is tense, he wants to move but he is stopping himself.

They both settle in an awkward silence.

"He looks... he-, is he-" Ilatr begins, until Jalila cuts him off.

"He has lost a lot of blood... but-", she breathes out heavily, as if to reinforce her words and thoughts, "-he is strong".

"He is strong," Ilatr confirms.

A slight metallic jingle causes Jalila to look over towards Ilatr. He is fidgeting with his ruby necklace.

He takes a deep breath.

Another wave of nausea washes over Jalila. The sky threatens to close in on her. She can feel the red is rising in her cheeks.

"ao'Jalila? I know this may not be the best time. But then... there is never a good time. And there probably won't ever be a good time. So I need to ask. Have you considered my proposal?" asks Ilatr.

Jalila can only hear the sound of the blood rushing to her ears. A sound much like that which comes from putting a shell to your ear.

She looks at her son.

The air that was still begins to pick up a bit.

Is that a western wind she can feel glancing past her face? It smelled bittersweet.

"ao'Jalila?"

Jalila's vision goes cloudy, her eyes go dull.

A sharp pain causes her spine to tingle.

She reaches down to the bite in her leg, but grits her teeth.

It is unbecoming to admit pain.

Ilatr follows the movement. He reactively moves to try to help, but is gently pushed away.

With some effort she responds.

"Ilatr, it's not that I haven't given your proposal thought. I have-".

She stumbles over her words as if she is drunk, "-and I want to say yes, but now is really not the time. I want to give you a real answer, I do and I will. But not right now."

Her voice trails off into the air like smoke.

Ilatr stares forward unhappily.

"I've heard this from you before Jalila," he says under his breath. He continues to stare forward petulantly.

What he doesn't notice is Jalila beginning to sway.

"Ilatr, don't be like this..."

Ilatr doesn't look at her.

"I know a lot has happened. Is happening. But that has made me sure of what I want and what I need. You. I need an *actual* answer."

He starts to walk on ahead quickly.

"Ilatr don't be like that. Wait... wait-".

Ilatr hasn't made it more than a few paces when the edges of Jalila's vision finally close. She feels a rush of hot air whip past her face as she falls to the dirt.

"a'Jali!?"

He is by her side within seconds. There is nothing he can do except hold her.

Jalila is feverish, her skin feels cold yet sweaty.

The wave of nausea has turned to a tsunami.

On the ground, she wretches first, then throws up.

"ao'Talia! akal'Mald come quickly!" He shouts.

Up near the front of the train Mald and Talia turn. Talia's hand moves to her mouth in reaction to the scene. Mald is already on the move.

"Mother! Look after a'Sha!" He shouts as he rushes over.

Before he can reach her, Ilatr has her lying on her back. He has taken off his scarf and is pouring water on it to lay on her head. She tries to get up, to move, but her movements are weak.

"a'Sha- I have to help him- I need to-" she repeats desperately.

"Stay down. You have to stay down," he responds.

Fear and desperation course through her.

Her vision is hazy.

A cold shiver runs through her despite the desert heat.

She keeps trying to get up but Ilatr keeps her down.

Jalila suddenly grasps Ilatr's hand.

"If anything happens. Protect him Ilatr. He is my everything-".

"Stay down," Ilatr says nodding. "I will. I will. But you have to stay down. You have to recover."

With her vision and consciousness fading she stretches out her other arm and tries to find her son's hand but it is too far to grasp before the darkness engulfs her.

"You have to recover-".

MALD

"We need another Suncover!"

Mald's own voice rings around his ears as he and his wife reach a'Jali.

"I don't think she should be moved yet. We should set up camp here-," Talia says.

"-It's only another few days ride to the Oasis," Mald says cutting her off, "and I don't want to stay out here in the open if I can help it."

Talia gives him an unsure look but doesn't fight the point.

Mald continues. "Let's get her ready to ride."

With that he gets up and calls his tribe to a halt until another transport can be drawn up.

Within moments a transport beside Jalila is emptied and converted to a person carrier.

As soon as it is ready Ilatr, Talia and Mald gently hoist her up and secure her in.

Mald pulls away, takes a deep breath and rubs his fingers. She has a cold sweat to the touch.

He turns to his second-in-command.

"Ilatr, what happened?"

"I don't know... We were talking and then she fell. She did look dizzy. That much was true... but I thought she was just worried about a'Sha," he responds.

"We need to keep her as cool as possible Mald," says Talia beside them. "If we aren't going to camp here then we must move as quickly as possible. Taking care of two isn't something we will be able to do for very long with the supplies we have."

She takes a damp cloth to Jalila's head, and looks over to a'Sha. Despite herself she shudders and shakes her head.

"Ilatr, go get a'Diwa. And find ao'Shiva. I need somebody here to help me with them."

The direct command shakes Ilatr out of his own head.

Ilatr nods.

"Yes, ao'Talia."

With a direct order he feels more confident and walks off with purpose.

Talia looks at Mald as Ilatr leaves, and nods in Ilatr's direction.

"Just *worried*?" She says. "The fool. Go find out what's turning in his head."

"You don't think I should stay here and help? Are you sure?" Asks Mald.

Talia nods again.

"For the time being I will be fine," she says, "but if we aren't going to set up camp then we need to be quick. *He* won't talk about what happened in full if I am here. Find out *exactly* what happened."

"You're right."

"I know. Now go quickly. The day is long, but our time is short."

Mald sighs, turns and catches up to Ilatr quickly.

"What exactly happened Ilatr," Mald calls out, "before she fell."

Ilatr speaks up as he walks forward towards the vanguard of the camel train.

"She looked distant. She almost fell when I caught up to her, but she kept her head strong. I should have realised that now wasn't the time to talk about it. I put too much pressure on her and she must not have been able to take it."

Mald looks at his second-in-command.

So *that* is what this is about.

"Jalila can take a lot more pressure than a simple conversation. Even that one. I think this is much more serious."

"Right. Yes. She is strong."

"...When she wakes up I'm sure she will give you an answer Ilatr."

Ilatr looks at Mald, then looks down to the ground ashamed of himself.

"It's been a long time," Mald says carefully as he spots Shiva and a'Kita on a camel with a'Diwa beside them, "-and she has never been good at saying what she means. But Ilatr this is not the time for that. Focus on her. What happened before she fell?"

"She was cloudy... And she had a sharp pain in her leg. But she didn't mention anything about it, she pushed me away when I tried to help."

They reach Shiva before the conversation can continue.

"ao'Shiva, a'Diwa, come quickly now. Jalila needs help," commands Mald.

Shiva gives them a concerned look.

"But... We just left her. I heard you shouting. She seemed fine when I left her a while ago. What happened?"

Ilatr answers.

"She collapsed. I don't know exactly."

Shiva looks from Ilatr to Mald.

"People don't just collapse out of nothing," she says with an edge to her voice.

Ilatr doesn't respond. He stands there stony faced, expression unreadable. He then slowly looks towards the East consumed by his own thoughts.

"What's wrong with ao'Jali grandma?" asks a'Kita, breaking the silence.

"She has gotten sleepy dear," Shiva says softly. Then she points at a'Diwa, "Come a'Di."

Shiva turns to Mald.

"Take a'Kita son. I'll go to a'Jali."

Mald picks up his daughter and puts her on his back.

Shiva gets off of the camel with a grunt of effort, but more grace than one would expect, and moves with haste towards Jalila. She slows only a few steps away and looks backwards over her shoulder. a'Diwa hasn't moved yet, instead she is staring with big eyes at Ilatr.

"Come on," Shiva says as she quickly walks back and grabs a'Diwa's arm.

a'Diwa yelps at the roughness.

"Yes, ao'Shiva," she says meekly.

They both make their way towards Jalila and a'Sha.

"Is Auntie going to be okay?" asks a'Kita from Mald's shoulders.

Mald looks towards the deep-in-thought Ilatr. He is muttering under his breath.

His second was an odd man at times, but he always wore his thoughts on his sleeve. If you knew how to read them. Clearly something is playing on his mind further than his own guilt.

Mald could tell that he was trying to figure something out, or rather, he seems to be trying to convince himself of something.

"No surely, surely not," is all Mald manages to catch.

"I'm sure she will be okay a'Ki," says Mald to his youngest daughter. "Isn't that right Ilatr?"

Ilatr doesn't shake out of his head but responds as if shadel touched. Outside of his own mind.

"Yes Fu'Aitauz."

Mald recognises the response, it is one that has been drilled into him over many years of warfare.

Mald looks at Ilatr seriously for a moment until a sharp grab at his head turns his attention.

His disposition lightens up as he tries to look up at his daughter on his shoulders.

"See a'Ki, even Ilatr knows she will be fine, and if *he* does then you know it must be true."

He bounces her on his shoulders as he replies and she responds with a giggle.

"Fu'Aitauz," Ilatr says somewhere off to his side. "Did Shiv-'Anu- did he give you any information?"

"I'm not sure what you mean," says Mald dismissing the question. "The lions are moving, but there have been no calls to arms as of yet. But there was another raid, he said. Something near the city, nothing too out of the ordinary. Southern 'Ifacho raiding southern merchants over the narrow water."

He stops to think.

"Though what I don't like is that I didn't know about it," he admits.

A shout rises up behind them towards the back of the train.

They both spin, hands on weapons.

a'Sha's thin, reedy voice carries on the wind.

"Mother."

SHA

"Mother."

Sha calls out in a thin voice.

His throat burns.

He opens his eyes and abruptly sits up in his transport.

Sudden pain courses through his body with the speed of a whip crack. His body gives out as the intense pain quickly forces him back down.

The fire-like pain is coming from his neck.

He grasps at it to try to soothe it, but it doesn't help.

Through the pain he can see above him is a dust-grey canopy.

Air.

Past that, sky.

Each breath feels incomplete.

He reaches out a hand to move the canopy so he can see the sky but it is too far.

His hand drops weakly down and hits warmth. He feels rough, short hair, and underneath, the deep breathing of a camel at rest.

He feels a tug on his other hand. Without looking he can tell whose hand it is. The shape of it he had known since before he could even remember. It was his mother's hand.

His eyes go wild with fear.

He doesn't know where he is.

He tries to call out again, but the pain of shouting forces him quiet.

He brings his hand up to his neck again and his mother's hand falls away.

He stares down, first at the blood on his hand and then to his mother in a suncover beside him.

His eyes focus on the wrapping covering the deep cut on her chest.

He sees the arrhythmic way her chest is moving up and down.

He can hear the crackle in her breathing.

His first instinct is to scramble to her, to make sure she is okay.

He tries to raise himself up but feels a firm but delicate dark-hand putting pressure on him to lay back down.

But he can't back down. His mother needs him.

Talia hugs him close and lays him down to stop him moving too much.

"Your a'ijd needs rest a'Sha. As do you. Now lay back down or you will fall," she says softly.

"-No, no I need to get to her. I-".

Sha tries to fight her, but sudden dizziness washes over him.

He tries to get back up but finds he doesn't have the strength, and after a few seconds of fighting, even that leaves him.

He allows Talia to lay him back down.

This time he can only stare at the covered ceiling of the transport, any slight turn of his head brings the fire back to his neck.

Talia makes sure Sha is down and returns her focus to Jalila, but doesn't say anything.

Sha's mouth tastes like sand and metal.

"Auntie?" He says, voice barely a whisper.

"Close your eyes a'Sha and try to rest."

"Auntie. May I -may I have some water?"

Talia nods and brings a water sack up to his mouth. He takes small gulps as he lays on his back. The water tastes off.

Sha coughs and tries to spit it out.

"There is medicine in the water. Try to drink it."

Talia forces him to take another swig which he swallows with a weak gulp.

"Is a'ijd going to be okay?" Sha says in a strained voice after swallowing.

"Your Mother is strong. She is strong," she says without looking at him.

Sha turns his head slowly to look at his mother.

Within a few moments he is on the brink of sleep, but fear quickens his breathing. He grabs hold of his mother's hand again.

"I don't want to fall asleep again, please."

As his eyes close he catches his auntie's eyes. The normally bright sea green are blood-shot and glassy. Her sleeves are wet with sweat and tears.

"I don't... to sleep again." He says, his voice a whisper.

Talia begins to softly hush him.

"All I see are those... those yellow eyes... and those rats scratching."

Talia keeps patting down Jalila's head. Until something clicks.

She looks to Sha. The darkness before sleep grabs hold of him.

He feels her hand over his forehead before it pulls away.

He opens his eyes as much as he can.

Talia's hand over his forehead, her other hand over her own.

She looks at Jalila and does the same.

Her reaction is different the second time.

SHA

SHA FINDS himself floating in the space between the bright and the shaded.

One moment he is caught behind the dark of his eyes, whilst in another he is in a tent that seems unbelievably large, and maddeningly constricting.

Images flash by his face and torches turn to starlight and then to eyes. In the distant desert, sand shifts to reveal marble feet on a plinth with nothing above it. The sea shore dissolves leaving naught but sand, and from a cloud of thunder comes blue and white lightning.

The sound of thunder forces his eyes open, but they close just as quickly.

The voices above him of Mald, and Shiva, and Talia all meld into one another.

Through the mist Shiva and Diwa arrive in the tent, Shiva huffing and puffing.

"Is he awake?"

His grandmother's voice comes from the distant sky. But there is no response he can hear.

Shiva gets her answer by looking at him.

"How is she?"

She then asks.

Jalila.

Sha opens his eyes at the sound of his mother's name.

He sees Talia shake her head.

Shiva, realising the seriousness of the situation, nods. A star losing her shine.

Sha loses grasp on time.

"a'Di dear, please go get us more water. We must keep Jalila cool," says Shiva softly but firmly.

"Yes, ao'Shiva," says Diwa meekly.

Sha can hear the slip of fabric falling back to the sand. Desert flowers never bloom in the dark.

Shiva watches Diwa leave the tent.

"How is she, truly?" asks Shiva again, more quietly this time.

"She is getting hotter and hotter," says Talia. "Mother… I think this might be more serious than we- I first thought. The cuts are angry but regular. This is coming from something else."

Through the darkness Sha feels a delicate hand on his head. The gentle breeze of the green sky gently soothes his hair.

Shiva nods.

"We need to know what exactly happened…"

The creak of a chair. Someone standing.

"When a'Sha awakes come get me."

The sound of fabric on sand again.

With that Shiva has left.

Talia continues to care for Sha and Jalila.

Diwa eventually, or was it immediately, comes back with water.

The sun, the moon and Godshome continue their cosmic dance through the sky.

MALD

OVERHEAD THE BLINDING sun with its cyclical waltz partner hang low in the sky.

Around the caravan where there was some soil before, now it is well and truly only sand.

At the head of the train stands Mald stroking his chin against the breeze and gazing out over the yellow-brown in the direction of his current home. Two dust clouds rise and hang in the air, but they are already slowly fading. Two of his outriders are riding full speed back to the Oasis. Despite the distance the blues of his tribe keep peaking through.

More omens.

Not only did the flash in Kiraj'it'Jalila bring with it the falling stars, but more have been spotted falling into *his* desert. If he were a more spiritual man, like his father was, he could believe it to be a sign that the shadel are opposed to his tribe's decision. That they disapprove of him and his actions.

But he couldn't wrap his head around any of that.

Maybe they cared, maybe they didn't.

Maybe they didn't exist at all?

The west and the north believe in one above all, even if they believed them to be different. In the north they were called the purifiers, fire was the sign of the divine. The west was different. They were people of blood and sacrifice. People of the earth.

His time in the east taught him about the many gods, with many aspects, the many shadel. There might be many more thoughts out there.

He didn't know. And if he didn't know something then experience had taught him that the mind must be kept open to all options, and not closed to all except one.

No, short answer was that he wasn't one for believing in omens.

Yet, even if he could reason his way out of it, he couldn't shake that deep gut feeling that he was missing something.

He strokes his chin and turns to watch his people.

They weren't on their transports anymore.

They have made good time on returning, but now they must let the animals recover and because of that they are slowly moving through the desert on foot beside their camels and silver-grey horses.

There was no need to wear them out by riding them unless speed was of the essence.

"You still want me to cover the trail out east Fu'Aitauz?" Says a tribesman appearing beside Mald.

"Yes Shala," replies Mald turning to face Shala, his fresh scar across his mouth still looking angry.

"Let's call it a feeling. I can feel the eyes of the shadel upon me. Something is about to happen and I don't want any surprises this close to the oasis. Stay out of sight, and send word when Shiv'Anu and the Dirauj are less than a days ride."

The scout with the scar, Shala, puts his hand to his heart and bows. Then he passes the reins of his silver-grey horse to Mald and easily gets onto the back of his camel. With a click on the reins he pulls away.

In the depth of the sea of sand the speed of a horse was not necessary during a scouting mission. The head of a spear is only needed when attacking, so the 'Ifacho saying goes, but the shaft of the spear, the camel, is what will support you."

Mald dabs his head with his scarf.

"a'Ijd. Please! This is too hard. I can't remember all of this."

The complaint comes from his son a little way behind him. He and his mother are in the middle of a lesson.

Mald's frown softens to a smile. No matter the length of time that they had been together, he can't help but be reminded of how lucky he was. He hadn't forgotten it of course. He couldn't, but something about her demeanour, her patience makes him remember their first meeting long ago.

The world and the hourglass may have turned, but nothing could make him lose the warmth he felt when his eyes fell on her.

He continues to scan his tribe. In the middle of the pack are the two transports holding Jalila and a'Sha. They are being cared for by a'Diwa, Shiva and the other tribeswomen.

The distraction flitters away as his mind returns to his present problems.

"Another attack," says Mald under his breath.

His initial anger at the tribesmen's report had subsided now. No point in anger towards the messenger.

Attack was a strong word judging from the report. The desert marauders had launched a raid on one of his returning traders from the south. In all honesty it was a miracle they had escaped, but his blue silks, not to mention the gold, were all gone.

He grits his teeth.

"Another attack against us. Another from the south. Years with no movement. First the horses and now the silk. Why?"

Everything had been quiet for so long…

It was like the build up before the Eastern rains. He could feel it. His grasp on the desert was slipping.

The question was to whom.

His eyes fall onto a'Sha's transport.

Could it be the other 'Ifacho to the west?

He spits at the thought. If it is, our little crown will meet his father much sooner than we thought.

He closes his eyes to feel the wind.

Maybe akal'Kali's spiritualism was right.

"Who are we a'Jhea?"

Talia's voice carries to Mald's ears. His mind returns to his son and wife.

a'Jheal has a considered look upon his face.

"Repeat the Kaogarea'[1]," she says calmly.

Mald sighs, not at his son but at the state of his own head. This feeling isn't something that can be figured out so quickly. His reaction was all he could currently control. He would need time and patience to think on it.

a'Jheal begins to recite the poem rhythmically, like the orators of old, *"I ask again, where is my home…"*

Mald lets the poem wash over him. Listening on some level but distracted.

He looks up as some red-crested oasis birds fly over head. The Maithane[2] were always a good luck charm to his tribe. The birds followed the tribe because their favourite diet was the dyed-blue silk worms that gave them the unique sapphire silk.

He kisses his sapphire ring. The birds meant he was nearly with his people, nearly home.

He looks around and can feel the hot, dry air on his face.

It's not the land that is home. It is his people.

a'Jheal pauses as his voice falters. They have caught up to Mald.

"Go on boy," says Mald.

a'Jheal wears a frown. He is trying to remember the end of the first stanza.

---

1. Kaogarea' [kao.ga.Rea.'] : used to refer to the 'Ifacho Kaogarea' or 'Ifacho Poem - lit. "kaogarea'" to want or desire
2. Maithane [mai.tha.ne] : Red-Crested Oasis Bird – lit. "Maith" Bird, "Ane" red

"*Free to choose where we roam, but ever to roam alone,*" he says unsure.

a'Jheal takes a breath and looks to Mald for a confirmation, but is met with a stony expression.

Finding no indication that he was correct from his father, he responds slowly to his mother's question.

"I can't remember the rest... We call ourselves 'Ifacho."

Mald thinks for a moment.

He nods.

"You are correct, in a sense. But that is just a name..."

He pauses.

"Carry on with the Kaogarea' a'Jhea, maybe there is an answer within it?" Says Mald.

a'Jheal scrunches up his face. He puts his hand on his chin and begins to bite the top of his knuckle.

The red crested oasis birds screech a high melodic note, filling the silent sonic space.

Shiva whispers to the wind from behind them, "*Now here I see...*"

He had to admit she was pretty silent when she wanted to be. Not too far behind them are Shiva and the train plodding along.

a'Jheal picks up on the help from his grandmother.

"*Now here I see where you roamed, old tents and the memory of them.*"

Mald shoots his mother a disapproving look, even if she was correct that he just needed a little nudge to recall the rest. He should have this all memorised by now.

a'Jheal finishes reciting the poem.

"Did you find anything in the words to help you answer the question?" Mald asks.

"Are we not 'Ifacho, Father?" a'Jheal asks frustrated.

"Our enemies call us 'Ifacho. But they know not the meaning, to them it is an insult. In their tongues it means homeless. Some also call us The Desert Lightning, or the storm from the stormless. But we are more than that."

He motions over the desert with his arm. "We are more than where we live-".

He tugs on his blue coloured head scarf. "-Or what we wear."

He pats the white mare next to him. "-Or what we ride."

a'Jheal looks up at his father.

"So it means we are free?" a'Jheal offers tentatively.

Mald motions for him to continue.

"And..."

"It means..." a'Jheal tries to recite a seemingly random part of the Kaogarea', "*And in the endless desert I see again the single stone. It's etching and scars fading in the sun and wind, but those children of the shadows remain.*"

A shot in the dark, sure, but there is wisdom in many places if you choose to look.

"Clever boy a'Jhea," says Shiva from behind them. She is still taking care of Jalila and a'Sha who are in the transport, along with looking after the girls, but was clearly listening from afar.

Mald, hearing his mother, nods. He isn't completely satisfied with the answer, but it was a start for sure. The point of the question is that it doesn't have an answer, it was meant to think about who you are, and who you want to be.

"Think more on it Jheal," says Mald slowly. "Reflection will give you a clearer answer, but that is a good place to start."

a'Jheal stares forward. His cogs turning, but frustration forcing his cheeks red.

"I think I don't understand your question Father. What was I supposed to say? Every answer I thought of, you said wasn't enough? Was I supposed to say we are the Children of the Shadows?"

He looks to his grandmother, then to his mother and lands back on Mald.

"What is the correct answer? What am I supposed to say?"

Mald can understand his son's frustration. It's the same frustration he felt when he was younger.

"My boy, you aren't *supposed* to say anything, you are free to answer with what you like-" Mald trails off as he hears Ilatr riding up close to the group from behind the pack. "-But therein lies the answer. We are the ones who are *free to choose where we roam, but ever to roam alone.*" Mald says quickly before Jheal can try to answer again.

"Alone," Mald repeats to himself.

The shimmer of recognition catches his attention. We alone are what holds the sands. We alone are the storm from the stormless. We alone sell the blue silk.

"Fu'Aitauz I need to talk to you-" comes Ilatr's voice.

Mald loses his train of thought.

Mald turns to his second-in-command with an unreadable expression.

Ilatr nods.

Mald's expression softens as he turns to his son.

"Ilatr knows who we are. And more importantly he feels it. It's a part of him as much as his hands or his heart. If you can figure out who we are and who you are yourself the sky will be coloured by it. You will be a man at ease with himself. Any decision you make will be sure. There is more power in knowing yourself, your people and your history than in any weapon. It will come, but it will take time. You will feel it too one day. We may be the children of the shadows, but really we are Roamers. We are free in not owning anything, and in turn having everything."

a'Jheal cheeks are burning. He opens his mouth to speak but Mald cuts him off.

"Now go help your grandmother, quickly now."

Ilatr, Mald and Talia watch as a'Jheal moves back to his grandmother and sisters tending to the injured. After he goes, Ilatr dismounts gracefully and lands onto the sand with a soft thud.

With a'Jheal out of earshot Ilatr finally speaks.

"Has there been any change?"

Talia shakes her head.

Mald responds, "she is getting worse."

"It's all happening too fast," Ilatr says before his expression becomes unreadable.

"I don't think she will... get better," says Ilatr, his words slow and considered.

Mald turns to look at his family behind them. Beside him the gears in Talia's head are turning.

"What do you know, Ilatr?" She asks. There is an answer there that she doesn't want to admit into her thoughts.

"It's... more of a feeling," he says, "and one which I don't want to consider."

His eyes search the sand for some solace.

"Yellow'd eyes... and gnawing rats..." Talia says under her breath.

Ilatr and Mald turn to look at her.

"Pardon?" asks Mald.

Ilatr suddenly comes to a realisation, one he seemed to be dreading.

"It cannot be. No. Not her. Not here. But it must be, it's here and it's just like across the water. That black ship that spreads the miasma, it has seized her-" Ilatr's voice falters. He has lost his composure.

"Talia. While you were cleaning her wounds, did you find any bite marks. Like the ones you would find from vermin."

Talia nods.

Ilatr breathes out slowly, steadily.

Mald closes his eyes, the weight of his sister's situation has finally settled on him. He hadn't wanted that answer to even be considered. The desert wind picks up masking the ever present clip-clomp of the camel's hooves.

"The black ships are here. I denied it and denied it but the truth will not be denied any longer. It's happening here as in the East. Everyone here will die if she doesn't take the walk."

"We can not be sure akal. We can not-" Ilatr says.

Mald signals for him to be quiet, the motion is a quick holding out of his hand and closing his fist. Ilatr's military experience kicks in and he stops.

"a'Jali..." Talia says, turns her back to them.

A wave of cheer and hollering rises from in front of them, washing over them. Deep in their own thoughts and without realising, their train far in front has been meet by their people.

"Keep them at a distance from the others," Mald says, "no one can be allowed to see them but us."

"a'Sha too?" Talia says knowing the answer.

"Even him," Mald responds. "The fate of everyone here rests on keeping this tribe calm."

Conversation over they walk the silent minutes forward, and despite the cheer and joy of a good return, none of the three feel the urge to say anymore.

They reach a final large dune and begin the climb, zig-zagging across it as they ascend and following in each other's compacted footsteps.

Reaching the top a wave of cool air flows around them. The Oasis wasn't large, from one side to the other would take a person on foot only half a day, but it was a gem. Adrift through the sand stretches out a green and blue gem against the yellowed-brown of the desert.

Below them are dozens of tents all laid out ringed around a central clearing, close to the Oasis but not inside of it. The camp had no walls. It needed none. The ocean of sand was more than enough. It would be packed up and moved before the season shifted. This was just one of many places the tribe would move to throughout the changing seasons.

Even so it held a special significance for Mald. The birds, the trees, the fruit all served as a gateway to old feelings. This was the place he first brought the silk worms from the east to, and where they developed the blue silks they are famous for; it was here where he became the Fu'aitauz, the horse leader and warlord of this desert.

It was the closest place to the Terkizcho idea of a home that he would admit, and they have made it back.

More than that, more than this place specifically, they have come home to the rest of their tribe. A few hundred or more of family and friends, spear-brothers and life-sisters.

Another roar flows up as Mald comes into view. The hair on Mald's arms rise at the sound.

The Oasis is prepared for an 'Ifacho wedding.

SHIV'ANU

Sitting atop his dark horse, Shiv'Anu shifts restlessly. Behind him, sitting lazily on their own horses are his troop of dull brown and sandy grey guardsmen. A couple of them are idly chatting, others are talking to the passers-by and traders here in the outskirts of the ruined old city.

Let them talk. Maybe they will scrounge up something useful, even if Mald wouldn't.

Shiv'Anu rubs at his tender, still red cheeks. His face was still sore even hours after the argument he had had with Tijjikauz. The pain wasn't too bad as the blow was open handed, and it lingered with mere stinging, but the blow to his pride... now that was what really got him.

A white rage threaten to surface at any moment, barely held down by self interest.

The question he had asked still hung over his head unanswered.

Why *was* that ship docked at his port?

He had accepted it when it docked under orders directly from Tijjikauz without question. A ship flying no colours was a curious thing in these waters, even if a war was brewing to the south, but he couldn't believe that a Black Ship would be allowed anywhere near an allied city. Especially not to the *gateway* to the ocean of sand, this lesser desert.

So he had come to hesitantly accept it here and had tried his best to lock it off alone in the port.

Out of sight, out of mind.

Shadel curse it.

Then the 'Ifacho incident.

It had forced him to acknowledge it, despite not wanting to. So he had to ask.

The first time, Tijjikauz had pulled rank and quietened him.

The consequence of repeating the question moments after had left the outline of the slap that still stung his face.

Shiv'Anu sighs.

He didn't like it and his pride raged in response, but he would find no answers right now.

With a smooth motion he swings his battered but well-cared for conical helmet and puts it back on his head and tightens the buckle beneath.

Behind him is Kiraj'it'Jalila's old city. Scattered around it are a few families and traders going about their daily lives.

Shiv'Anu looks around.

"However did I come to this," he says under his breath, "Governor and all."

He looks over to his small guard troop. They were a standard patrol, here to show a presence more than anything else. Usually he wouldn't even have come along, but Tijjikauz had requested it.

A pebble falls from the crumbling walls as some children jump around on top of them. They meet his gaze and quickly duck to cover.

In the distance, over the hill tops, a light shower of dust and blue emerges.

Looks like some of akal'Mald's 'Ifacho seem to be returning to the city. Mald must be ready to talk.

Looking back over to his patrol he notes that their armour looks very similar to the dull brown stones around him.

Of course they were. His men's armour was made for war, to surprise invaders, not to protect the people.

That should change.

He would change it. His job was defence, not war. At least not any more.

He realises he is staring when one of his men shifts uncomfortably.

They carried themselves well, their backs were straight on their horses. Clearly these were men that enjoyed their elevated position, but these Terkizcho warriors weren't his men, not truly.

Maybe he should buy some of that 'Ifacho blue to add to his guard. That would allow them to be seen.

He shakes his head.

"What is it Sir?" Asks his second-in-command by his side.

Shiv'Anu rests his hand on his sword in one easy motion. It's a movement developed by years of training.

"I was thinking about adding blue to our uniforms..."

He notes that the second isn't really listening.

"It's nothing important Kirajauz," Shiv'Anu says with a sigh.

Kirajauz sits back in his saddle and relaxes.

"Everything alright, soldier?" asks Shiv'Anu.

Kirajauz doesn't respond. Instead he continues to idly fidget with the reins of his horse.

Shiv'Anu clicks his teeth with an audible, palpable annoyance.

This Kirajauz notices.

He stops.

"It's nothing," he says.

He catches Shiv'Anu's eye.

"It's nothing. Sir." Kirajauz says again, correcting himself this time.

Shiv'Anu nods.

To the air, to his horse, to himself, he begins talking.

"I remember these deserts from my youth, you know." He taps his horses' neck and continues. "You are a good horse. Not as fast as Mald's silvers, but bigger. Braver. Like the war horses of the west."

Kirajauz puts his hand on his weapon.

"Sir."

Shiv'Anu takes no notice and continues speaking.

"When akal'Mald and I were younger those horses saved us more than once. Those silvers I mean. Strong beasts, like lightning. And he was the only one with the purebreds."

Kirajauz repeats louder this time, "Sir."

"What soldier?" Shiv'Anu says irritated. "Yes I have seen them. But they should pose no threat. Look at the colours. Blue on white. They are Mald's men. If anything we should be getting prepared to help them."

He stops abruptly. The hairs on his back rise.

It couldn't be, they looked like they were charging.

Mald wouldn't, would he?

His are one of the most well known fighting forces under the Dirauj. He protects the sands. His tribe would be finished if it lost the Dirauj's patronage.

In the distance a yell is raised.

He heard it, felt it even. It was a war yell. The hair on the back of his neck stands on edge, as it does when the world feels wrong.

He draws his sword.

"'Ifacho! Raiders!" A woman shouts near him.

The woman's scream startles his horse, but he manages to keep it under control.

"Get back behind the walls. Now!" He commands her, but she is scared. Her husband practically drags her backwards.

Another 'Ifacho war yell is raised, the sound isn't the one he remembers from his youth.

Something isn't right.

Loudly one of his men shout out.

"The 'Ifacho have come back! Mald the War Dog has turned on us!"

Shiv'Anu holds out his hand and closes his fist, but the Terkizcho warriors continues to shout. He clicks his teeth again. These men need to be trained his way, but it's too late right now.

"You!" Shiv'Anu points towards his man who is yelling. "Round up who you can and get back to the walls now! We need reinforcements on those walls to break the charge."

The Terkizcho stops and nods. Then he reins in his horse and turns back to the city and rides.

"Get behind the walls, Mald's 'Ifacho are attacking," the Terkizcho yells all the way back.

Shiv'Anu turns back around. There was something in that young soldier's eye that he did not like and his shoulder, it was weak on the reins, as if it were broken. Did the fool fall off his horse or something, why had he not said anything?

"Men! Lines!" Yells Shiv'Anu in response to that strange war yell.

His Terkizcho guards show off their training. They quickly and easily form up in response to his command. Kirajauz takes position near the back.

Shiv'Anu clicks again in annoyance. He could never abide by Terkizcho tactics. The leaders should fight in the front.

The sapphire blue enemy approach at speed, dust rising behind their silver-white horses. The entire effect of brown-gold sand behind, white speed and blue silk reflecting off of metal spear-heads and sabres resembled upside-down lightning striking the ground.

Running into that storm was suicide, but he had to break the charge or else the 'Ifacho would run without any barriers through the city and be gone before they could muster a defence.

He steels himself.

"If that is you Mald, by the shadel I will take you to Godshome with me if it's by my dying breath."

He raises his pole arm with a yell and spurs his horse forward.

Behind him the other men follow suit.

Shiv'Anu focuses on the storm in front of him as he rides headlong into it. A part of him, a part he hated but also longed for, couldn't help but admire the charging band.

Once upon a time he had been a part of it.

He spurs his horse harder, hardens his heart and lets out another yell, which is picked up by the Terkizcho behind him.

In the golden desert Shiv'Anu and his golden-brown guard clash with the 'Ifacho storm.

MALD

AT THE EDGE of the Oasis, in the last lonely tent before the endless desert, emerges Mald looking depleted. He strikes a solitary figure alongside the solitary tent set a distance away from the others.

The hollows around his eyes give them shadow.

He rubs them.

He was tired. All his energy these last few days had been spent on returning to the Oasis as quickly as possible-...

-The tent flap behind him is caught by the wind and whips itself open to briefly reveal Jalila and a'Sha.-

...-whilst also trying to conceal the tribe's potential destruction from them. Many were with him and Ilatr in the East, and the others knew all the stories. The miasma spread with devastating speed if left unchecked. His people would demand purification. Everyone and everything that the two had touched would be burned. If he could keep it quiet, they could instead take the walk.

A whimper comes from his sister within the tent behind him. She is tossing and turning in pain. a'Sha is lying on his side, breathing deeply and sleeping even more deeply.

Mald looks up to the cloudless blue sky. More falling stars streak across it. They were getting hard to ignore, but he wouldn't let himself be distracted by falling stars in the sky.

Watch the arrow in the sky and miss the scorpion at your feet.

His hands unconsciously form fists and then release. He is breathing heavy to hold in his emotions. Between the breaths, and beneath his feet, the sand rumbles lightly.

"Father?" Comes a'Jheal's young voice.

Mald glances upwards.

Shiva and his son have stopped short of him. Shiva is holding a'Jheal close.

Mald blankly stares at his son for a moment. Then looks behind towards the tent.

"I- They are fine, my son."

Mald softens his expression as he looks to his mother.

"Why aren't you both helping a'Di get ready? The wedding is upon us."

"He wanted to see a'Sha... and a'Jali. I tried to stop him, but..." Shiva says as she takes her hands off of a'Jheal and spreads them wide. "He needs his Father to help him understand-".

"I do understand. They have to take the walk. I know. You told me, but why can't I see them first," a'Jheal says, his voice straining through his emotions.

Shiva puts herself awkwardly to a'Jheal's level to explain.

"The walk. Our ancestors were the first walkers but..." she pauses trying to think of how to explain it.

Memory touched his heart. His father had been the one to explain the walk to him. Every 'Ifacho must take the walk at least once in their life. It was a chance to touch the edge of the infinite sand, open their heart to the shadel and return with their wisdom.

But Mald knew they would not return.

Shiva knew.

How could they explain the truth of it to a'Jheal?

"Here listen," Shiva begins again. "It's *because* they have to take the walk. Something happened to them when a'Sha ran away. And they might have brought back something, and well, we can't be sure yet. Until we are sure, you just can't see him."

"But- but why, I won't stay long. I promise I'll only be a moment."

"ao'Shiva it's alright. I'll take him. Go back and make sure a'Di is ready-".

Mald's jaw clenches.

"-Tijjikauz will be here soon."

With a subtle gesture he beckons his son to follow him as he turns and walks into the desert towards a large overhanging rock.

a'Jheal doesn't move.

Shiva ruffles his hair before turning away to go back towards the centre of the camp.

For a moment a'Jheal is left alone between the two. He turns to catch a glimpse inside the tent, but feels the distance growing between him and his father. After a moment of hesitation he quickly follows after him.

The boy catches up to his father at a run. They walk together for a few paces in silence until they reach the overhang.

Mald sits at the edge and with a slow welcoming gesture offers his son a seat.

a'Jheal sits beside him in an easy motion.

"Father do-," a'Jheal begins but Mald holds out his hand and closes his fist quickly. It's the motion for silence, the same motion every 'Ifacho warrior ingrains into his heart.

a'Jheal quickly silences himself.

He is a good boy. He listens well, and takes orders well. He will be a fine storm-rider one day.

They sit and watch the desert swirl.

After a few moments of stillness a'Jheal speaks up.

"Did you really say a'Sha could raid with you?"

Mald looks at his son.

Then back to the desert, a light smile crossing his face.

"I did," he responds softly, "and I offer you the same proposition with the same question. How would you raid a city with powerful walls?"

"I'm not sure," says his son in his usual, more considered manner. "I think I would wait until their men are outside?"

Mald smiles at his son and gives a slight laugh.

"Very quick and very wise, little lion."

Jheal smiles at the praise.

"Very wise. And it's the answer I came to also and many before you. But it is also not *quite* what I asked."

"Oh," says Jheal slightly dejected.

Mald hugs his son.

"My hope is for neither you nor your cousin to come up with the answer that I have seen... But I think it is one you will need to know before it is too late. Think on it some more though. You and a'Sha-" he stops himself at his nephew's name.

"Have I ever told you the story of our Kiraj'it'Jalila and Parfi'at?"

Jheal nods.

"Yeah," he says, "but... tell me again."

Mald smiles.

Telling stories was something of a legacy for his people, and he was carrying on the tradition he and his forefathers had passed onto him.

He begins in a melodic voice. One could say that it was a more developed version of the one Jheal was trying to use while reciting his poem. One that could inspire.

"Kiraj'it'Jalila and Parfi'at were once the twin gems of our side of the Eastern Eye Sea. A home for the homeless. It withstood the Western Eye conquerors. They stood even amongst the shifting sands of the Eastern Dirauj-".

Jheal interrupts, "-but now the walls are crumbling? Wasn't it the Eastern Dirauj that did that?"

Mald considers this before his response.

"The Eastern Dirauj has committed many tragedies. For they

have grown and died and grown back again many, many times. But at the beginning the twin gems at the maw of the sea were one of our gathering places after the flooding of the Great Dam in the south. One of many such places that still stand.

However they stood *against* each other more often than not. They stood even against the Once Ao'Dirauj[1] of the Desert, that fearsome Woman Fu'Aitauz."

Movement behind them cause the two to turn.

Talia is walking towards the tent with new water. Her face is shielded as if a sandstorm were raging, leaving only a gap for her eyes.

Jheal tries to get her attention but Talia doesn't see him.

Mald continues on, turning back to the desert.

"However, in the Desert, at the old Aiwash[2] a new Dirauj arose, an 'Ifacho Dirauj-".

Despite his focus on his mother, Jheal interrupts the story.

"-We have no 'Ifacho Dirauj father. Only Fu'Aitauz. How could there be an 'Ifacho Dirauj?"

Mald smiles.

"Ah so you figured out who *we* are then?"

He ruffles Jheal's hair.

Jheal looks confused, but pleased at the compliment.

"Yes, *we* have no *true* 'Ifacho Dirauj. That is a cursed title. It is a contradiction."

Mald looks up towards the dancing planets as a swirl of green and purple flickers in the sky between them. No matter how many times he has seen it throughout his life seeing it again never fails to amaze. The light meant another green flash this evening.

He continues.

---

1. Ao'Dirauj [ow.di.row.] - Queen without the connotation of being subservient to a king - lit. "Ao'" Female, "Dirauj" king
2. Aiwash [I.wa.sh] – Camel Stables – lit. "aiwash" camel stables

"This 'Ifacho Dirauj is now known as Diraujcho[3] and he lashed out with fury on all fronts, and gathered our 'Ifacho kinsmen together. Even the Western *Fergilna*."

That last name Mald says with venom, visible disgust crosses his face.

"He was, at first, a man who embodied all of our ways. Free. Fierce. He was a new lion come from the depths of the ocean of sand. His raids became legends, East and West, and he raided throughout the desert and fertile South."

Jheal tugs at his scarf, "was he in the Blue also?"

Mald shakes his head.

"No, the Blue is *our* family's symbol. I was the one who created that, and the world knows *us* for it."

Mald smiles a toothy grin and ruffles his son's hair.

"And you shall continue it. The Storm 'Ifacho will only continue to grow."

Mald pauses.

That feeling that something is clicking into place surfaces.

"Blue silk..." he repeats.

It clicks.

"They raided us for the blue silk, but not for any gold." He says under his breath.

"Are you talking about the other night? When they stole our horses?"

The question brings Mald out of his thoughts.

"No son, this was-... *What did you say?*"

Jheal is taken aback, and worry crosses his face. Mald doesn't understand Jheal's fear, then he realises the tone he used was one that usually indicates anger. Mald reassures his son with a smile.

"Do you know who raided us?" Offers Jheal tentatively.

---

3. Diraujcho [di.row.cho] - False king, or usurper - lit. "Dirauj" King, "cho" negative, or Not King

"I'm sorry son. No," says Mald, "you said *when they stole the horses*. Where did you hear that?"

Jheal doesn't know what to say, he seems torn for some reason.

Mald repeats, "where did you hear that?"

Jheal looks down to his feet before answering.

"a'Sha told me not to tell anyone. He- he said that you'd get mad."

Mald sighs.

"I won't get mad at you-".

Jheal doesn't look convinced.

"-or at a'Sha. Just tell me."

Jheal still doesn't look convinced.

"Hear me now. You are going to be the one to take over this tribe one day," Mald says, "and you will always have my trust, no matter what you do as long as you do what you feel is right. But right now I need you, as a man, to trust me. To trust me as your Fu'Aituaz. I won't get mad at you or a'Sha but you must tell me what happened."

Jheal seems reassured at his father's statement.

"a'Sha told me at the market place before-..." Jheal looks torn again, but he persists. "He said that he woke up the other night at a noise, like- like a tent's leather being ripped. The raiders were cutting the leads to the horses. He said he was scared and couldn't move. But then he saw a few of them taking the leads and stealing those horses, while others let some loose... and then- and then-".

Mald urges him on softly.

"Go on. Go on Jheal."

Jheal continues in a strained voice.

"Then they started cutting and ripping our greys. He said he couldn't stand it, but that he was too scared to move. One of the mares reared up and kicked one of the raiders after she was stabbed, he said. Sha heard a crunch, he said. And the raider's arm looked all sorts of disfigured, backwards, he said. But then they ran.

They took their own horses and ran and just left the mare there to bleed."

Mald's head was spinning. They stole his horses, and they stole the blues, this confirmed it.

But who? Someone was trying to impersonate him, but who?

With a start he realises Jheal was still speaking.

"Sha said he saw she was in so much pain. He said that he had to, that it felt like the right thing to do. He had to end it for her. He said it was the right thing to do. He-"

Jheal bursts out into tears.

Mald embraces his son tightly.

"It's alright. Everything is alright. He did the right thing. I'm not mad at him. Or you. Not at all. You were both men after that night. A man does what he feels is right, for that is all the Shadel can demand."

The boy and his father continue their embrace.

"Thank you for telling me Jheal," says Mald after letting the tears fade. "You were very brave to speak on his behalf. Sometimes people are too stubborn to speak out the truth of a matter, even if they are in the right."

They separate.

Mald looks to the sapphire ring on his finger. Then takes it off, removes a strip of leather from his pocket and combines them into a necklace. He hands it to the boy.

Jheal accepts, but looks confused. Without a word he looks at his father questioningly.

"It's something for you to keep," says Mald, "you trusted me. So. I'm giving this to you, to show I trust you."

The boy looks at the ring, and then back to his father. Then he dons the necklace and stares at it.

"Will Sha still really have to take the walk?"

Jheal's question cuts the moment.

Mald is at a loss of words. He opens his mouth to speak but stops. He tries again, but stops again.

A cooling wind blows from the oasis, and the sun begins to cast more and more orange light into the sky.

"Would you like me to continue with the story?" asks Mald, avoiding the question.

Jheal nods.

"Where was I? Yes. The Dirauj of the Desert. After his name became known, The Dirauj of Kiraj and Parfi'at, Tijjikauz's grandfather, invited him to his house as a treasured guest.

"Great was the bond that grew between these two. It seemed as if we might have a true 'Ifacho Dirauj. A man that could withstand the Three Lions around him.

"Yet, after a time he grew complacent in the city, as does any 'Ifacho that stays in one place too long. The West, the Fergil, signed a treaty with him. Now he was only to attack the East. Then the Eastern Great Dirauj offer him great riches to stop his raids.

"Now he was only to attack the South, but the Southern Lion was old and decrepit and not worth his time. All he had left was to raid his kinsmen's home.

"He raided the Twin Cities. Breaking the bond between the two 'Ifacho. It is a tradition that is not so far from our own, truth be told." Mald adds with a grin.

"But not any more, now we are offered greater riches to protect it and the land around it than we could get by raiding it. And we gave our word. We do not break our word without good reason.

"But the Dirauj of the Desert. He did not leave after the raid with his riches as is proper. No. He crowned himself Dirauj of all the 'Ifacho, killed Tijjikauz's grandfather and forced Tijjikauz to flee to our desert.

"This Diraujcho wasn't just paid by the Eastern Dirauj to stop raids against his lands, but also to strangle the Twin Cities. The Eastern Dirauj was jealous of their prosperity and wanted their land. But he didn't know that as 'Ifacho our wealth is cultivated by being free to roam. Those that own the land, end up being owned by that land.

"The Diraujcho settled and was just like all the rest that settle, just like Tijjikauz's grandfather. The hourglass turned, and swallowed him."

Mald stops himself there as he feels a sad look crossing his face.

He looks back over to where the tent that houses a'Jali and a'Sha lay. Talia exits the tent at the same time. She doesn't spot her husband. For a moment she looks to the ground deep in thought. Then she hurries off in the direction of the centre tent.

The pyres of the oasis are lit. The change that has come over the Oasis finally sets in. Torches have been set up and a large fire has been lit nearby. The effect was similar to the fire bugs of the swamps on the furthest shores of the East Eye Sea.

Images of the dead being dragged through those swamps flood his eyes.

He takes a deep breath and turns around to look out across the sky.

With effort he continues.

"The Twin Cities revolted, were punished, then revolted again and again until one was burned so completely that not even the shadel could return up to 'Ifa Shadelna.

"Tijjikauz returned to his 'Ifacho roots, and we kept him hidden. But he was bound to the land of his fathers. With our help, and his own promises of gold and the help of the new Eastern Dirauj, we drove that Diraujcho out of Kiraj. Tijjikauz became who he is today, shackled to the Eastern Dirauj. And we secured his west for gold, becoming his spear and shield against the Fergilna.

"He lost who he was, as did the Diraujcho. As do the people in the cities lose who they were."

Mald finally looks down at his boy.

Jheal is nearly asleep and has his head in his father's lap.

The Sun and its dark twin, known to the 'Ifacho as 'Ifa Shadelna, are setting over the sands.

"You won't forget who you are, will you little one?"

a'Jheal half turns in his sleepy state.

"Did Sha's father fight the Diraujcho as well?" He asks.

Mald strokes his son's head, but at the question he hesitates. A flash of anguish fleets over his face and leaves a sadness in his eyes. He looks from his son, to the tent and back to his son.

Then sighs.

"We fought many times. But yes. I had to... fight... his father. They did not agree with being paid to secure this land. Said it felt too much like submission."

He says even as the boy is losing his battle against sleep.

"We are family a'Jhea, and we will always be. Nothing can ever change that," he says quietly.

a'Jheal is asleep.

Mald lays his head down on the stone and covers him with his scarf. He stares at the boy, and a feeling, like a well being filled and over-running comes over him.

How could he leave them for another war?

Leave them behind for someone else's glory.

He couldn't.

He had paid his penance, redeemed his promises.

He would fight tooth, nail, claw and sword to stay right here with his family in this moment.

Behind him a rhythmic pounding begins, the goat skin drums have been brought out in the central encampment.

Like a poison darkening that well, remorse and guilt dyes the feeling a deep shade of purple.

It hurt him, and no matter how much he reminded himself that duty came first, that his daughter would be better off in the care of a man like Tijjikauz, that his tribe would be able to continue their way of life, that they would not take part in the next war... the deal had forced him to cut a part of his heart, and to shut down his mind.

The wound to his heart threatened every second to take his breath away.

He looks back over to the desert and the setting sun. The desert wind blows a slight chill causing the hair on the back of Mald's neck to rise.

"akal'Mald? The wedding preparations are nearly complete."

Mald recognises Ilatr's voice immediately. He turns to find Ilatr and another one of his tribesmen, Shi'Auz, a colossus of a man, as wide as tall, standing behind him.

True to his word, in the centre of the camp a great black wedding tent has been set up. Surrounding it are the tribe's prized white horses and many camels.

His people have begun to gather. As the festivity preparation is nearly complete the tribesmen and women are becoming more and more jovial, fermented horse milk and fermented honey flows between jug to mug and into bellies, leaving red-cheeks in its wake.

He catches Ilatr looking at the tent housing Jalila.

"Ilatr…" Mald says. "Come when you are ready."

Ilatr shakes himself out of it.

"Tijjikauz has arrived," Ilatr says simply, in a tone belying the storm of emotions that must be raging through him.

Mald nods and gets to his feet.

"Shi'Auz, take my son to his mother's tent. He must get ready for the ceremony."

The big tribesman nods.

Mald and Ilatr watch him scoop the boy up as if he were a doll and take him towards the tents.

"Come Ilatr," says Mald, "let us go out to greet him then."

DIWA

The young, golden-skinned and raven-haired Maithanai lets Diwa's blue and gold wedding veil fall over her face and takes a step back to inspect her work.

Diwa huffs and looks away, sulking.

Maithanai put her hands on her hips. Then she takes a step forward, lifts the veil and cusps Diwa's face in her hands.

"You are beautiful my cousin," she says, "but don't sulk."

Diwa huffs again, but meets her gaze. There is a fire in her eyes.

Maithanai chooses to ignore the anger.

"Almost there." She smiles, "almost done. And then you shall be ready. And your mother will be happy. And your grandmother. Don't you want to make them happy?"

Maithanai doesn't let Diwa respond, but then Diwa didn't think that she was looking for a response anyway.

Maithanai lets go of her face and puts her hand on her shoulder.

"Before you know it you'll be one of the most powerful women on this side of the desert. Aren't you excited? You won't forget your Maithanai will you?"

Diwa doesn't respond.

They look at each other for a moment.

Maithanai had pretty eyes.

The thought catches Diwa off guard, and in response her anger flares. Why couldn't *she* take my place? She would be much better suited than I.

Maithanai takes her hand off of Diwa's shoulder and looks around, either taking no notice or being completely unaware of Diwa's anger.

Suddenly Maithanai panics.

"Shadel save me. The dagger. Have you seen the dagger?"

Diwa looks around concerned.

"No a'Maitha. I haven't. Are you sure you haven't misplaced it?" Diwa says with perfect innocence.

"I know it was just *here*," Maithanai says pointing to a cushion on the ground.

"I don't think so," says Diwa standing up, her blue, black and gold wedding garbs brushing against the carpet with a silky sound, "I didn't even see you bring it in. Maybe you left it in your tent?"

Maithanai shakes her head but says "Maybe, maybe."

She spends a few moments looking about for it before huffing.

The entrance to the tent flaps down with a dusty whoosh as she walks out.

Diwa stands in the centre of the room and waits for a few moments listening out for her cousin to be well out of earshot. Then she nods to herself.

"What do I need, what do I need," she mumbles under her breath as she quickly runs over to where her bedspread lay unmade. She whips away the top cover, and grabs the plain ivory handled, curved silver dagger she had hidden earlier.

She throws the veil on the bed and her black hair falls to her shoulders.

"I will not have my freedom taken from me," she says conviction coursing through her words, "and I do *not* accept this."

Within a few steps she is at the entrance of the bridal tent.

Without warning, ao'Shiva strides in.

Diwa stops, statue still, eyes wide.

ao'Shiva's eyes are closed and she is holding the bridge of her nose.

"a'Maitha. I know you are busy but could you please help me and prepare some tea."

ao'Shiva opens her eyes.

Diwa can't move. She is petrified; her veil thrown on the bed; the dagger holstered to her belt scarf; her earlier confidence shattered.

Maithanai is nowhere to be seen.

ao'Shiva puts the pieces together at a speed Diwa didn't think she could at that age. ao'Shiva breathes out slowly and evenly. It was the sound of a sealed pot over a fire with a small hole in the top, and it was about to blow off.

"I specifically told Maithanai to keep an eye on you. I don't need this right now. My head is killing me. I told her too, while I had to take care of a'Kita and a'Jhea, to stay here. And now-" ao'Shiva's voice raises. "What? Are you trying to run away too? You saw what happened to a'Sha when he tried to run. Do you know what could happen out there to a girl alone?"

ao'Shiva is breathing heavy. Diwa has been stunned into silence, standing as she is in the middle of the room.

"a'Sha-" continues ao'Shiva, "it's him. That little boy has gone and given you ideas. It's his fault. It has to be. Look what he has done to this family. That son of a *Fergilna*."

Diwa's face goes red, the fear being replaced by a white hot anger.

"How dare you! How dare you blame it all on a'Sha. It's no wonder he doesn't feel like a part of this family. No wonder he is always acting up. Running away. No one ever takes him seriously. No one ever gives him any responsibility. He is just always told to do, and to do as he is told. And *you* are always awful to him!"

ao'Shiva's response is quick and loud, "I. Am. Not. Granddaughter! And you will mind your tongue and your tone unless you want to make this situation worse than it already is. You aren't talking about him, so don't you dare use him as some sort of weapon. *You* are talking about *yourself*. If you cared about him you wouldn't be so childish. If you cared about anyone but yourself *you* wouldn't be so selfish."

"Selfish!" Diwa responds indignantly. "*Selfish*? All my father ever talks about is the *freedom* of this tribe. All the Kaogarea' ever says is that we aren't to settle. We are *free to choose where we roam*. Where can I ever be selfish? Where is *my* freedom to choose where to roam?"

ao'Shiva takes a deep breath, her face is crimson.

"That dagger on your belt, do you even understand what it means?"

Diwa rolls her eyes.

"Here we go," she says.

ao'Shiva continues, "that Faijh a'ilatr[1] was a symbol of this tribe from before even *I* was born. It is to be presented to akal'Tijjikauz as a symbol of our joining. *You* are that joining more than the Faijh. You are the one who will keep us, like that Faijh, protected."

"Well maybe I don't want to keep you protected," Diwa retorts throwing the dagger to the ground. "Maybe I don't want to be that joining!"

"Stop being so childish!" Shouts ao'Shiva again. She takes a step forwards and a loud crack echoes through the tent as Shiva slaps Diwa.

Diwa falls to the ground clutching her cheek.

"Do you think you are the only one who had to do *this*? *This* is our duty. Me. Your Mother. Jalila. It is us who keep this tribe free. Not the men who run off and die in their silly wars. No. *You* will *not* break that tradition."

Dust hangs in the air.

Diwa feels tears roll down her cheeks as Shiva towers above her.

---

1. Faijh a'ilatr [fai.jh.a.il.at.r]: side small sword, or dagger held on the side - lit. "Faijh" side, "a'" lesser, "ilatr" sword

Slowly the red seems to escape her eyes as Shiva realises what she has done. She takes a step back and sits down, then puts her hand to her mouth and bites her top knuckle.

"I'm sorry a'Di," she says softly. "That-That was uncalled for. That was wrong. I'm sorry."

Diwa doesn't look at her. She continues to face away from her, tears rolling down her cheeks.

Shiva exhales slowly.

Maithanai appears at the doorway.

"Away a'Maitha," says Shiva not looking at her and waving her hand dismissively.

Maithanai looks from Shiva to Diwa and back again.

"Oh. That's where the dagger was," she says as she backs away quickly.

Shiva ignores the comment.

"It won't be so bad. Once you get used to it. Once upon a time I was just where you were," Shiva says to Diwa's back. "As was Talia, as was a'Jali. I know how hard this is."

Shiva looks up to the ceiling of the tent.

"But Tijjikauz is a good man. Him and your father were close once. Tijjikauz was hungry. He was driven. He was smart and ruthless. But he was gentle too."

Shiva sighs and looks towards the entrance.

"Those were dangerous days, and they led to even more dangerous days. But we thrived. And you will thrive beside him-".

-A large rumble, similar to a soft earthquake, shudders through the ground and the tent.

Diwa gets to her feet.

"What was that?" she says quickly.

"The shadel shaking the ground. Nothing to worry about I'm sure-".

-Without warning a sudden gale wind hits the tent. The entrance whips open almost horizontally as dust and sand fly in.

Diwa and Shiva are caught looking at the entrance as the flap opens. They both close their eyes and cover their mouths quickly, but despite their best efforts, begin coughing and wheezing. Within seconds the aftershock passes as quickly as it came.

Her eyes burn as Diwa rubs them.

As she regains her vision she sees that there is a man standing at the entrance coughing with his back to them.

She rubs her eyes again. He is tall, with grey-specks in his hair and skin the colour of deepest night.

He is still facing the desert as he stumbles backwards into the tent. He turns away from the dust to try to find some sort of shelter.

He rubs his eyes to try and see where he is and with his vision slowly returning sees Diwa and Shiva.

With the grace of a cat he descends to a bow.

"ao'Diwa," he says staring at the ground, then with a motion as smooth as the bow he looks up and stares into her eyes.

Truth be told Diwa was frightened by the man.

The corner of his mouth turns up in a small smile.

Shiva coughs with dust still caught in her throat.

The white-haired man turns to Shiva, "and of course you must be ao'Shiva."

He gazes around the tent, and then seems to realise where he is.

"Oh my dear. I seem to have ended up where I wasn't supposed to." He speaks with a light tone as he inspects the tent. "That sudden storm breeze seems to have blown me off course."

The white-haired man gives another cat-like smile. Then something like a light-bulb goes off in his head. He turns to Diwa and kneels before her, grabs her hand and kisses the back of it.

"ao'Diwa, I am Nguahealo."

Diwa is taken aback by his brashness, and his unusual accent.

"I don't recognise that word," she begins, "where is-".

The white-haired man grimaces.

"My apologies, in your language it would be closer to Jhealo. But you, ao'Diwa, may call me whichever suits *you* best."

"Nguahealo-," Shiva begins.

"Please feel free to call me Jhealo," Jhealo interrupts, "that name is more apt in your tongue."

"Nguahealo," Shiva continues unamused. "You are not welcome in this tent at this moment. Diwa is getting ready for the Dirauj."

"My apologies to the ao'Dirauj," he says in response, without seeming to detect the shortness of her tone.

"Would you prefer if I leave?"

This question he directs towards Diwa.

Shiva gives a single chortle.

"You are foreign to our ways Terkizcho, she is not ao'Dirauj."

Shiva begins to herd him out, "Now I must repeat, you are not welcome-".

"*I* say you are welcome," says Diwa.

Shiva stops suddenly, her body tense. She turns her head slowly as she looks from Jhealo and then back to Diwa. A clear annoyance blossoms in her eyes.

"I apologise ao'Diwa," he says with a smile. "I am still learning your ways. I meant no disrespect."

Diwa rubs her eyes and smiles sweetly.

"Jhealo, are you from the city?" She asks.

Jhealo pulls away from Shiva gracefully.

"I am, ao'Diwa. Have you ever been?"

Diwa nods in approval.

"Just a few days ago in fact, we were gathering supplies for this wedding. Tell me, is it always so lively in Kiraj'it'Jalila?"

A puzzled look crosses Jhealo's face.

Then realisation strikes and he chuckles.

"Oh. You were speaking of Kiraj'it'Jalila. I misunderstood, please forgive my lack of this tongue. I come from the city of Shanomzeh[2], up near the Heart of the Eastern Dirauj."

His eyes light up.

---

2. Shanomzeh [sha.nom.zeh] : Ul-Terkizcho (from the language of the Terkizcho) lit. Settlement Big, or City

"The greatest city in the world," he adds.

Diwa looks at him wide eyed, almost forgetting to close her mouth.

He seems not to notice and carries on.

"Yes and I suspect you shall be going there frequently after you are a wife of akal'Tijjikauz. He spends most of his time there in fact. It's nothing like Kiraj'it'Jalila."

He looks at Shiva apologetically.

"My apologies my ladies," he turns back to Diwa with a laugh, "but Shanomzeh makes Kiraj'it'Jalila look like nothing more than a few market stalls around a tower."

He laughs deeply and Diwa finds herself laughing with him.

Shiva fidgets with her dress. She is not used to being ignored. And she does not like being ignored.

Diwa and Jhealo laugh again.

Shiva didn't catch that last sentence.

"ao'Shiva, you wouldn't mind getting us some tea?" He says, then looks at Diwa, who giggles again. "Or maybe some wine? I can't seem to see any anywhere?"

Shiva has had enough.

"Jhealo, leave now, or else I do not know what Mald-" Shiva looks him up and down with disgust "-and, more importantly, akal'Tijjikauz will do if he finds his wife-to-be alone with such a man as *yourself*."

Jhealo looks around the tent again seemingly oblivious to the threat.

"Oh ao'Shiva. I do apologise."

He bows to her. The platitude reinflates Shiva somewhat.

"But I'm sure it'll be no worry," he continues. "I mean, akal'Tijjikauz did send me ahead to check in on the preparations after all."

Shiva's hands fall to her sides and she squints at him.

Diwa can feel her frustration. She can't help but find some joy to it.

Jhealo looks again to Diwa with a smile.

"Everything looks fine here, wouldn't you say so?"

Diwa is clearly enjoying herself.

"I would," she responds. "You say I'll be in the great city? Truly?"

Jhealo finds a mug on the ground, and gives it a blow to remove the dust and sand. He waves his hand as he talks.

"Why yes, I do believe so. The others are there after all- ao'Shiva, I don't mean to impose, but that divine wind has seemed to have left me severely parched. Would you mind?"

He pushes the mug towards her.

"Yes. Shiva. Would you mind?" Says Diwa sweetly to her own grandmother, pushing her own mug towards her.

Shiva can't believe it. She grabs the mugs with a disgusted look.

With the mug out of his hand Jhealo immediately ignores her again and puts his full attention on Diwa who turns and accepts it.

Shiva stands in the corner, mugs in hand.

Then without a word heads towards the exit.

Out of the corner of her eye Diwa watches her grandmother walk out and a ping of empathy rings through her.

She looks at the ground and bites her lip.

"Is something the matter ao'Diwa?" Jhealo says noticing her discomfort.

Diwa shakes herself out of it and smiles at him.

"No akal'Jhealo. No. It is a matter I shall deal with later. Now, I would like you to tell me more about my husband to be. Tell me about akal'Tijjikauz."

MALD

STANDING on the ridge of a dune, looking out towards the eastern horizon, Mald and Ilatr are watching the Dirauj of the Twin Cities and his convoy come ever closer. The tribesmen can feel the rumble of the horses' hooves even from this distance.

"The Dirauj has come with more men than I expected. Must be more than a hundred guardsmen with him," comments Mald.

"He still thinks quantity is more important than quality," responds Ilatr. His level tone belies the disgust with which Ilatr has for the minor dirauj.

Mald agrees with a nod but stays silent. He knew better than to engage with that point. Instead he changes the subject with a more jovial tone.

"A large wedding party behind him also. I wasn't expecting so many though. Well. No matter, it's a good thing we got extra of everything. This might have been too many to feed and host otherwise-".

Without warning a sound like the largest rockfall comes whooshing, like a tide of air receding before a great wave. It takes both men's breath away. The men both spin-

-And are greeted by a truly massive cloud of sand. The wave

knocks both men off of their feet and down tumbling to the ground. They go down hard and roll down the dune.

As quickly as it came the sand wave washes out over the two tumbling tribesmen towards the approaching army. Mald catches a glimpse of the army as it turns before the wave hits. The last thing Mald sees before his head is forced down is the entourage's rough form as it splinters.

Through instinct more than thought Mald curls himself as tightly as possible on the ground. For moments that feel like hours the sound is all-encompassing. Until quickly, like a snap the sound begins to die down.

Sound that was always there, but masked by the dust begins to drift to his ears. Horses whiney, and people shout and scream as the sand breaks upon the entourage.

The wave continues until it finally dissipates further into the horizon.

"Ilatr!" Shouts Mald, sand dripping off of him as he gets to his feet.

Mald swings around and sees a small mound rising.

Ilatr groans.

"Yes Fu'Aitauz. What in Shadel's name was that!"

Mald runs over to help him.

The men have no time to think. Without warning hooves and swords on shields signal the coming of the Dirauj's forces. With a yell the horsemen of Kiraj have surrounded Mald and they have their weapons levelled at the two men.

Both 'Ifacho withdraw their weapons, Mald his curved cavalry sabre, and Ilatr, his heavy metal mace. They put themselves back to back without a second thought.

Adrenaline courses through Mald as he cries a war yell, "Come on then!"

Suddenly a voice booms out above the horsemen.

"Down! All of you! Now!"

The Terkizcho force responds instantly, the horses neighing as they are forced to a sudden stop. Spears still levelled at the 'Ifacho.

"Weapons away! All of you!"

Mald can hear the blood coursing through his ears. That shock wave hit his senses, but did not dull them.

The 'Ifacho don't sheathe their weapons.

Out of the fighting force, flanked on either side by his elite golden-brown Terkizcho warriors, a muscular man appears before Mald and Ilatr. His hair is dark and speckled with silver. In this setting sun, the red-gold light makes it look like embers on a fire.

Mald could only picture the child as he was, many years ago.

Here is Tijjikauz, the Dirauj of the Twin Cities, and Minor Dirauj to the Eastern Diraujzeh[1].

Mald and Ilatr face him like the trained soldiers they are.

He is garbed in crimsons, golds, and blues. The setting sun makes him and his men's armour blaze gold. Despite all of his pomp however his stance is that of a warrior. He, like his close guard, is well trained and impressive.

Mald's blood runs hot, but he doesn't lose composure. He stares at Tijjikauz, and after a moment, sheathes his sword back.

Ilatr follows.

Tijjikauz theatrically lets out a slow, loud, breath and laughs, cutting the tension.

"akal'Mald, my old brother. This desert is always strange. But *that* was nothing normal."

Tijjikauz turns to one of his captain.

"Take twenty and go find the source of that divine wind."

His captain bows. Then with a quick signal readies to ride with a small detachment.

"Oh and captain. Be sure to make it back *before* the festivities," Tijjikauz adds with a grin.

---

1. Diraujzeh [di.rauw.zeh] : Greater King – lit. "Dirauj" king, "zeh" Terkizcho word meaning greater.

His captain nods and rides off.

"May you find shade," Tijjikauz says turning to face Mald.

"May you find shade," Mald responds in a level tone and with a bow.

Ilatr follows.

Mald inspects his long-lost shield brother as Tijjikauz turns to Ilatr. Time had been kind. He has seen his fair share of turns and Godshome's wanderings, especially for a warrior of his experience.

"And may you find shade, my cousin," Tijjikauz says bowing again to Ilatr.

"May you find shade also, Dirauj," says Ilatr with ice pouring out at every word.

Tijjikauz raises an eyebrow at the title, seeing the insult baked within it.

Mald begins to talk quickly before Tijjikauz can retort.

"Today is a joyous day," he says, "'Ifa Shadelna has come to grant us it's blessing-".

Mald looks back over his shoulder towards where the sand wave came, "-or at least certainly a sign."

Mald coughs. The wind still had his breath. He noticeably does not look at Ilatr.

"Come. We must be away in case another wind comes. We have already completed all of our preparations," Mald says trying to distract the Dirauj from Ilatr's slight. He moves close and puts his arm on Tijjikauz's shoulder in an attempt to lead him away.

Mald catches Ilatr's eye, who looks down to the ground ashamed of letting his emotions get the better of him. Even just barely. Mald almost imperceptibly nods his head at his second-in-command. The movement is slight, but the message to Ilatr is clear. Calm down.

Despite Mald trying to lead him away, he feels resistance as Tijjikauz holds his position.

"Cousin," he asks Ilatr with a hurt note in his voice. "What is the matter?"

Ilatr doesn't respond.

"Well a'Ila?"

Mald looks towards Ilatr and shakes his head.

Tijjikauz licks his lips.

"Nothing." Ilatr says, trying his best to keep his voice neutral.

"-Cousin." He adds trying to keep the word from seeming as an afterthought.

"Come on Ilatr," Tijjikauz says happily but with a malicious glint in his eye "-lighten up. It's not often that *our* people have a wedding this important. A union between *our* small house and Mald's."

"Finally," he turns to Mald and continues, "we shall be brothers truly. By blood rather than just by arms. Brothers..." he laughs to himself. "Well, I mean brothers in spirit at least. In reality I shall call you my new father-in-law."

Ilatr can't find the words.

Tijjikauz catches Ilatr's eyes again and sighs.

"Ilatr, it is not good to dwell."

Ilatr begins to breathe slow and heavy to control his emotions.

Tijjikauz laughs.

"Oh lighten up cousin. This is to be a joyous day. The shadel have willed it with that sign. We must celebrate. Although on the subject of linking our families. ao'Jalila is still a widow, no? I know how much you liked her when we were younger. It has been so long since we have met. Have you finally gathered the courage to ask her hand?"

The mention of Jalila's name finally causes Ilatr's short leash to snap.

He tries to grab at his mace, but Mald gets inbetween him and Tijjikauz, stopping him immediately.

Around them the elite guard have their swords levelled again. They take no chances.

Tijjikauz laughs loudly.

"Calm," says Mald softly to his friend. "Calm."

"Oh it's just a bit of fun Ilatr," says Tijjikauz sweetly.

Ilatr stops himself, but the strain of his self control is almost visible.

"Go see to the girls, Ilatr." Mald says to him. "Make sure they have everything they need."

A moment of uncertainty from the two 'Ifacho.

Ilatr nods. Then turns and begins to walk away towards the tribe.

"Stop," demands Tijjikauz.

"I want you to be here while we discuss-", he then looks at Mald sympathetically. "While we discuss the little matter in Kira-j'it'Jalila."

"What is there to discuss, son-in-law?" Mald's usually even tone cut with anger.

"Not yet your son-in-law, Mald. We need to talk about what happened a few days ago. Ilatr, stop right where you are. I heard you were on the ship... How are you feeling?"

Tijjikauz's eyes seem to gather shadow as his tone deepens. "What happened?"

Ilatr turns.

"One of our boys was playing on the dock, and he was attacked. He was unharmed. Nothing more, nothing less," Ilatr says calmly, belying his internal anger.

Mald holds out his hand across Ilatr and begins to speak.

"We thought it best to do what we are known for and come back to the desert-".

Tijjikauz stops him.

"I had to smooth over the-", he speaks carefully, "-the incident. The Eastern Dirauj's law demands an eye for an eye. But I have some leeway within my own Kingdom. Having said that he imparted the importance of his *special* ships and his *special* officers... But I must admit I had no knowledge of what that ship was. Now, looking back, I realise Shiv'Anu should never have let it be docked at my port. He has been disciplined in response."

Tijjikauz turns back to Mald and smiles. He claps Mald on the back with a soft thud and softens his voice, "and, you know, how could I forget our history. We are family, aren't we?"

The rhetorical question hangs, causing Mald to shift his feet uncomfortably.

Tijjikauz doesn't seem to notice the discomfort. He moves in to them as if speaking a secret. He keeps his voice low, just for their ears.

"Mald, and you Ilatr, I have a question I desperately need an answer too. I need your help and your horse. Will you join us in war once again? Your vanguard is invaluable."

Mald and Ilatr don't respond. The question has come too quickly. First that divine wind, now the question? Mald didn't have time to prepare.

The sun has completely set, but the last light still colours the sky.

A Maithane flies overhead, singing a tune of high-pitched notes. But the tribesmen don't answer.

Tijjikauz repeats the question.

"Well? Will you join our war in the south?"

Tijjikauz leans in closer.

"What's your answer?"

Mald takes a deep breath.

"The death ship. Did you know about it?"

Tijjikauz looks out over his desert. He shrugs.

"I knew nothing. Shiv'Anu knew about it, but refused to tell me."

Mald asks again.

"The black ship. I haven't seen something like that since our last war in the East. And never here. I won't let my horse and my men, my tribe, die to be fed to those evil ships."

Tijjikauz shrugs again.

"I don't want this war to last longer than it has to. Your horse will bring their defeat faster. Maybe so fast the Eastern Dirauj won't even consider using the ships."

Mald and Ilatr digest his words and their implications.

Talia approaches from the camp during the momentary pause.

She bows at Tijjikauz as she reaches the group.

He smiles a mischievous grin and as is proper of a Dirauj, bows deeply to her.

She responds with her own tilt of the head.

She glides towards Mald, and whispers low into his ear.

"ao'Shiva needs you."

Mald nods as she pulls away. He turns to Ilatr and motions for them to go. Then finally turns to Tijjikauz.

"akal'Tijjikauz," he says. "I had thought our preparations complete, but there is a matter I must urgently attend to. There is still much to do before the ceremony. Please, come when you are ready."

Tijjikauz responds with a smile at Talia.

"Of course, do what you must. We will recoup and shake the sand from ourselves. And on the question I posed. I don't need an answer right now, but I will need one soon."

"One more thing," Tijjikauz says looking over in the direction of the camp. "Has Shiv'Anu arrived yet? Or Nguahealo? It's not like them to be late. They should have been here by now."

Mald looks confused, but quickly replies.

"No akal'Tijjikauz. I have not seen Shiv'Anu since we left Kiraj. And I'm not sure if we have greeted anyone by that Terkizcho name. But I shall go check presently. We have left a section for your train and party on the border of the Oasis. Come let me lead you to your preparation tent."

Tijjikauz hums in acceptance. He nods towards his captain, who in turn lets out a commanding shout. Around them the guardsmen dismount. Then, loudly, the entire convoy moves slowly towards the Oasis.

SHA

SHA'S EYES open in a daze caught within the soft orange glow of firelight. Outside night has fallen. Firelight is seeping through the thin weave of his medium-sized tent.

A dull repetitive thudding is trickling to his ears from outside. It takes him a few moments to realise it is the beating of drums, and not just his own heart.

A flicker of pain from his neck. He moves his hand up to his throat. It is painful, angry, but has stopped bleeding. His hand falls back down to his side as he stares up into the ceiling.

He turns his head absent-minded-

-And sees a shadel, a wraith, made real.

Fear tightens his throat as he chokes back a yell.

Sudden recollection hits him like a hammer as he recognises his mother.

She is lying down on her back, drenched in sweat and shivering despite the lasting heat of the day.

He sees beside her is a bucket filled with her blood and bile.

He tries to call her name but his voice doesn't come out.

He tries again, but his voice is shaky and nearly a whisper.

"a'Ijd?"

Jalila turns her head over to look at Sha, and as she does her yellowed eyes tears up. The bandage over her eye begins to leak.

Despite himself, Sha lets out a whimper of fear and recoils.

"I love you, my little crown..." says Jalila softly, her voice strained and reedy.

Sha's fear dissipates leaving immense sadness.

He hears a noise outside and in reaction to it draws himself inward.

The flaps of the tent are drawn backwards as three cloaked figures enter. They are deep in discussion, talking quickly but in hushed tones.

Sha instinctively pretends to be asleep.

"He is a snake," hisses Shiva. "Fu'Aitauz, we must be very cautious. And we must be quick. The wedding is already underway. I do not believe she will try to run again, but you know how she is. I must go back to her quickly. I do not trust that Jhealo... but at least he has found a way to make her mind settle."

Sha sneaks an eye open. He doesn't initially recognise them, they are completely garbed, except for the eyes. The lack of recognition is only momentary. He quickly makes out who each one of them are by their shape. Mald rectangular, long, a pillar of a man. Talia, curved, elegant, and Shiva much like her son, another pillar.

The three of them turn their gaze on his mother.

The drums outside change and bang a quicker beat.

"We must not halt this," says Shiva. "Diwa must marry the Dirauj. Jalila-".

Mald cuts her off, "-I know we mustn't stop this. It *is* too important. We stand in this moment on a knife's edge... But Mother, she is your daughter. He is your grandson. They are sick. *But* if they can speak they deserve a choice."

Talia's voice now, softer than Mald's.

"I found no marks other than sword strikes on a'Sha. Shadel willing he may not need to take the walk. But what do you suggest ao'Shiva. That they both make the walk? Now? Before we have a chance to deliberate over the matter? Can we not wait until the morning and my a'Di-" She falters at her daughter's name "-until the bride has left to her husband's home?"

Mald responds.

"I don't know if we *can* wait until morning. I have seen this before my love. It *is* too late. During the last war the same miasma was used by us and against us… It- It is inhuman. It will spread too quickly. It will kill. And it will mean the destruction of all of us. No, we must not wait, but-" Mald's conviction falters, "but-… neither can I do anything without *her-*" he directs the comment at Jalila "-agreement."

"Inaction?" Shiva responds. "Inaction is the course you want? Look at her Mald. I love my daughter, and maybe- *maybe* my grandson can be saved, but *she* will not live like this. She doesn't even know what's happening right now-".

Sha's eyelids flutter. His breathing intensifies.

Did he just hear what he thought he did?

"-She would be better if we were to end her suffering here and let the shadel care for her through fire and flame-".

"No!" Sha screams as he jumps up to his feet and moves to protect his mother, standing over her like wolf protecting cubs.

Talia and Shiva are caught statue-still.

Mald, as if by reaction more than thought, grabs Sha by the collar and throws him roughly away from her.

Sha hits the ground some paces away. Agony courses from the cut in his neck as it starts to bleed again.

He writhes on the floor clutching at it in pain.

Despite the pain his little voice calls out.

"No! How could you-. No!"

Pleading and looking at each one, his eyes are red with tears.

Mald doesn't raise his tone as he speaks.

"Mother, I will take responsibility for the boy. I trust your judgement," he says, it comes out as forceful and unstoppable as a glacier.

Shiva opens her mouth but quickly closes it before speaking. Mald is not to be argued with at this moment.

Mald kneels down and puts a hand over the boys head.

"a'Sha. No- Sha," he pulls down the scarf covering his own face. "I will treat you as an adult. You deserve more than that. But what I need you to do for me right now is to act like one, and try to see the bigger picture."

Sha can't stop sobbing. His eyes have focused on his mother now, and he can finally see her properly.

She is sick. Very, very sick.

"a'Ijd, no. Please, get up. Please."

Sha doesn't truly hear Mald. Everything is as a distant planet compared to his mother.

"Sha," repeats Mald.

Sha still doesn't hear him. He can't take his eyes off of his mother.

"Sha."

Mald kneels, then sits the boy up and forces him to look.

He meets him eye to eye, man to man.

His tone softens.

"Sha, you don't deserve what is happening right now. The shadel have a habit of throwing sand in our eyes when we least expect it. But being a man is about doing the best you can even when the world isn't being fair. Right now you need to be strong. So be strong. Be strong for *her*."

Sha nods slowly and meets his gaze.

JALILA

IN THE DARK of the fire lit tent and through a hazy eye Jalila sees her a'Sha nod.

"Come. Take my hand and come with me," Mald says with authority as he gets them both to their feet.

Through the haze of pain she could see that her son was in shock. And it broke her heart.

Mald pauses at the front of the tent.

"I love you a'Jali," he says with a brief painful look. "This should never have happened. I'm sorry."

a'Sha lets Mald lead him out of the tent.

Jalila looks up to the dark corners of the ceiling. Rings of light colour her vision. It felt as if she were under water, sound and light played with her senses.

Beside her she can hear that Talia and her mother are the only ones left in the tent with her.

A silence falls over them.

Shiva bends down over Jalila.

"My daughter, I- I am truly sorry. I would do anything to trade places with you," says Shiva slowly and tenderly, "but we can't let you stay here."

"She can't move ao'Shiva," pleads Talia who appears over her shoulder. "What do you expect us to do, we can't- we can't-".

Talia trails off.

"If she can't move," says Shiva with authority, "then we must take action. We know what this is. Mald. His father. Even Ilatr have all told us what this- this Miasma is. The breath of the shadel is poison. And we can't let it take all of us."

Talia is taken aback, almost as if she were forced away from the situation. She knew that Shiva was right. That much was clear from her body language but she couldn't find the words to vocalise how badly she felt about it.

Shiva walks towards the back side of the tent and begins to rummage through a chest with care. She doesn't let any article of clothing touch her skin as she moves it away with her sleeve.

Talia is stuck to the floor, staring at her mother-in-law.

"Please don't do this," Jalila mouths softly, but neither of the other woman can hear her.

Then with a creak from the chest Shiva finds what she was looking for and slowly straightens up. A green glint shows she has found Jalila's dagger.

"We need to burn this tent to burn the miasma, daughter." Says Shiva as she slowly, so slowly and so softly pads across the room. "And it would be better if you weren't here to feel it."

She is breathing heavy, as if she has just run for miles. She slows her breathing. It becomes deep and steady. She reaches Jalila and sits down next to her.

"I don't know if you can hear me," Shiva says. Her voice is breaking as she speaks. "My a'Jali."

Shiva leans closer to her daughter and as she does so her usually stern demeanour breaks away, leaving tears behind.

"I remember when you were so little... You- you always leapt head first into any challenge that lay before you. Whether it was the waves or the west. Our a'Sha got that from you- and when you returned to us... You may not think it was, but it truly was *the* happiest day of my life."

She leans back and readies the dagger above Jalila.

"My a'Jali. I want to give you the choice. I do. But I know you can't respond. You would do the same for me. And it would be the right thing to do. We put the tribe above any of us. I know you would do the same but... I'm so- I'm so-- I'm so sorry."

Talia panics.

"ao'Shiva! Please! Don't!"

She leaps at Shiva and grabs at the dagger. Talia's hands grab the only parts she can. One hand wraps around the bladed end. The other finds a hold on the cloth of Shiva's wrists.

Instinctively Shiva pull the dagger away.

Talia lets out a shout in pain as the blade cuts through her fingers, then into her sleeves and into her arms. She falls back a few paces and lands on the floor holding her hand.

Shiva stumbles but finds her feet. She left standing, looking over the women.

"I don't want to do this Talia. I don't want to- I don't want to! I love my daughter."

She looks to the ground. The hold on her dagger loosens as she sees the blood dripping from the shocked Taila.

Shiva makes a decision and her grip on the dagger tightens.

She looks at Talia with resolve and tears.

"If the choice is my daughter or everyone, you, Mald, everyone. The entire life of this tribe... I won't allow everyone here to die."

From behind her a soft croaky voice picks up.

"You don't have to choose a'ijd," Jalila says.

Shiva and Talia spin to look at Jalila. She is sitting upright in the bed with her arms supporting her. Her legs lay uncovered, they have green-yellow gangrenous marks all over them. Her feet and the tips of her fingers are black with necrosis. Her upper body is an angry red and yellow, and swollen.

"A choice like this would haunt you a'ijd, no matter how strong you are. I will walk..." each word is a struggle. "I will walk."

The two women are in shock.

Talia sprawled on the floor and holding her bleeding hand to her chest.

Shiva drops the dagger with a full-bodied sob.

"My a'Jali-" she repeats again and again between tears.

Jalila gets up and wraps herself in a blanket like a shroud. She walks slowly over to the tent cover. Each step feels like an age, solely fuelled by her determination and willpower.

"Take care of my little crown" she says softly before she leaves the tent, "... and keep a'Di safe."

The tent flap falls behind her as she walks out.

Musicians from the tribe and from Kiraj are playing goat-skin drums, pipes made from old wood and the insides of goats, along with high-pitched and intricately carved wooden violins.

Men from all over dance with curved swords, while whips bang and beat on the drums along with the musicians.

Twirling and spinning with dizzying speed women pass around an ivory-hilted ceremonial knife to each other in a circle, all the while dancing with the men.

Despite the assault on her senses Jalila doesn't truly see or hear anything. Her focus has been completely pulled into just putting one foot in front of the other.

She walks away from the tribe and out over the desert.

The cold desert air pricks at her inflamed skin. Jalila wraps her shroud around her as she walks.

She looks from the shadowed sand to the sky and sees the other world. That's the direction she must go.

A sound finally breaks through the pain and determination. She turns in a daze and sees her son and her brother by the overhanging rock.

For a brief moment a memory of the distant past comes back to haunt her. The memory of her little brother and father sitting up on another overhang before they left to war.

She loses her breath as she locks eyes with her own son, and all the pain and fear seems to dissipate.

"I love you a'Sha," she says with all the strength she can muster.

The sound is barely a whisper as it leaves her lips.

Godshome flashes a bright neon-green light and it wraps the world in its green shawl.

In the distance a war-yell picks up from the wedding and the singing turns to screaming.

But Jalila doesn't hear it.

All she hears is the heart beat of a distant ocean beating upon the sand of a distant shore.

SHA

Sha and his Uncle leave the tent in silence.

The world is a blur of sound and vision, and Sha can't find the ability to understand any of it. Each fire light reminds him of his mother's yellowed eyes which meld and blend with the sailor's eyes on the black ship.

Each high-pitched sound of the instruments reminds him of the haggard breathing of his mother which blends into the memory of the scratching of the rats on the boat.

Every memory blends and swirls around in his head.

The scene unfolding in front of him is the opposite of the macabre within the tent. Out here there are joyous, on the edge of reckless, people dancing and singing without a single care in the world but the next bang of the rhythm.

Kiraj guardsmen and their convoy of women are dancing with the tribespeople.

People move with the firelight. Dance with it.

Musicians from the tribe and from Kiraj are playing goat-skin drums and small wooden instruments that seem to move and breathe. Men with curved swords and whips bang and beat along with the musicians.

In a circle around the fire women pass around an ivory-hilted knife to each other all the while twirling and dancing with the men.

The scene whirls and moves in front of his senses, yet he can't register it.

Mald leads them towards the outskirts of the celebration. Towards the overhang a little way away.

Through the fire and the flames the scenes of festivities leave long black dancing shadows over the tents and walls.

Without being able to understand it the shapes and light and movement is more chaotic than Sha had ever seen before.

And it scared him.

Unconsciously he reaches out his hand to Mald's.

As his hand touches Mald's, he feels his Uncle recoil.

Sha's hand hangs in the air.

His Uncle's grabs his with renewed strength, as if he were angry with himself.

Sha lets out a relieved breath.

They walk slowly around the edge of the ceremony.

Mald pauses and looks around from the overhang.

"Fu'Aitauz," comes a call from nearby. Moving quickly out from the darkness of the desert comes one of Mald's outriders. Behind him a little distance away is the outrider's horse standing with his head down. The reins lay hastily discarded on the ground beside his feet.

The outrider reaches Mald in a cloud of sand.

"Catch your breath Tilau'a," Mald says.

The outrider, Tilau'a, nods and bends over for a second as he lets out a long breath, then quickly looks back at Mald. The man is short, even for one of the tribesmen, and wrapped in a blue shawl. In the darkness it allowed him to blend into the night sky.

"We found where the star fell, Fu'Aitauz. We found the source of that divine wind. It's not too far from here. The sand around it has been turned to glass. But we had to leave when the Dirauj's men got there."

"You found the star?" Asks Mald quickly.

"There were lights inside, akal. And sparks. It was like small green and red firelights from within the star. To be completely honest it looked like- well it looked like some sort of-…"

The outrider bites his lip.

"Go on," says Mald.

"It looked like a transport inside. Almost like one of our trains. But it was empty."

Sha squeezes Mald's hand. Distracted Mald looks down to his nephew. Then back to Tilau'a.

"Be quick Tilau'a. You went inside? Did you find anything before you were forced out?"

"I'm sorry akal, that's when the Dirauj's men got there. But I left Milaud there out of sight. He will be able to give us more information."

Mald nods his head. He feels Sha's little hand squeeze his again.

"Too much. It's too much at once. Why would they force you out? I must think. Go back to the star- caravan- whatever it is, but keep out of sight. I want to know what the Dirauj is doing, and what he seeks."

Tilau'a nods, and turns to his horse. He makes it a few steps before hesitating. Then he turns around with something like a box wrapped in his hands.

"Also, we- we found something," he says as he unwraps the object.

It was unlike anything Sha or Mald had ever seen. The box was hard, rough, yellow and made of a material Mald had never seen.

Tilau'a hands it to Mald.

"I don't know what it is Fu'Aitauz. I haven't opened it. But I took it before we were forced out."

Mald lets go of Sha's hand and takes the yellow box delicately. It has two latches on either side of a handle. He wraps his hand around the handle and lets it lower down by his side.

Then Tilau'a nods again and quickly goes back to his horse.

Sha watches Tilau'a ride back into the desert a distance, then looks up at his uncle.

He tugs at his uncle's clothes.

Mald looks down at the boy with an unreadable expression.

"Whatever is going on out there can wait. It's all too much. But you, Sha, are what matters right now. So come," Mald says as he holds out his hand.

Sha takes hold of it and lets him lead them.

Quickly they reach the overhang.

"Sit," Mald tells Sha, who does. Then Mald gets down to one knee in the sand in front of him. He gently places the star box upright by the rock.

Delicately Mald looks at his nephew eye to eye.

Sha stares back at him with eyes still glassy and red.

Mald hugs Sha close and tight.

Sha's arms slowly rise up to embrace his uncle and he begins to sob.

"I know Sha... I know, it's alright" says Mald.

"She is going to be okay, right?" Sha says between taking in large gulps of air. "She'll come back from the walk? She can't- she just wouldn't- she wouldn't leave me."

They pull away and Sha notices that he isn't the only one with tears in his eyes.

Mald looks at his nephew for a moment before sitting next to him on the rock. Mald brings him in close again.

Behind them, carried by the wind, the music thumps dully in the background.

They both look at the moon and Godshome.

"It's nearly time for the flash," says Mald pointing to the other world.

Sha doesn't respond, lost as he is within his own head.

Mald rubs his own eyes.

"Look up there. Look to 'Ifa Shadelna. This only happens when we come this close."

Sha rubs his nose with his shirt. A brief pulse of pain comes from his neck with the movement. Thankfully, as raw as it is, his neck had stopped bleeding now.

"Do you know what 'Ifa Shadelna is?" Mald asks.

Sha doesn't respond to his question, so Mald continues.

"It's the place where spirits go. A home they return to after they leave our home. You were too young last time it came this close. But every seven years we get so close we can touch each other, and then we depart to meet up again in seven years."

Sha snivels.

"a'Jali... your a'ijd," Mald's voice breaks a little, and he begins to tear up again. He can't quite bring himself to say it. "Sha. Your a'ijd has to go. She has to go up... there."

He points up.

Sha follows his hand and looks at Godshome.

"But she will come back right?"

His Uncle's lack of a response is response enough.

"Uncle. No, she can't. I don't want her to. She can't," Sha is pleading and fighting at the same time, "I can't."

He turns away from the sky.

And sees his mother.

She is wrapped in her dark shroud and walking towards the other planet. Her feet unsteady in the shifting sands.

His voice leaves him before his body can react.

"a'Ijd!"

Before realising it he is on his feet. He runs a few paces in her direction until Mald's arms wrap around the boy.

Sha kicks and screams as Jalila turns her head around to them.

Suddenly the sky lights up a bright neon green, a light like the Northern Lights but far, far more intense.

At the same time, a war yell picks up from the wedding.

The singing turns to screams while the light wraps up the world in a ghostly hue.

DIWA

Diwa sneaks a peek out of her wedding tent's entrance.

She was told that the bride was not to be seen until she was to take the walk towards her husband-to-be. The walk was symbolic, she remembered, with her father's dagger in her belt and a shroud over her face. It was to resemble how her people first traveled the desert. After leaving the stone and becoming the children in the shadow of it, the children of the shadow.

She lets out a mirthless laugh.

Each and every 'Ifacho, from the furthest west to here the furthest east, had to learn that silly little poem by heart. She wanted to learn more. She wanted to go to the sea and see beyond it.

"Diwa," comes Maithanai's urgent voice from the dark behind her, "you can't be seen yet. It is not proper."

Her hand grabs Diwa's shoulder and drags her back into the dull orange glow of the tent.

She swings around with indignation at being handled so roughly.

"You will call me ao'Diwa from now on, Maithanai," says Diwa, that same indignation coursing through her voice.

Maithanai sucks her teeth before responding.

The Hourglass That Swallows You

"After tonight maybe, but until then, my *cousin*, you will still be a'Diwa to me."

Diwa huffs and moves back over to her preparation area. Without a word she kneels down and lifts up her veil to take a sip of her sweet tea.

Maithanai takes a seat next to her and takes a sip of her own tea.

"It's not long now cousin, not long," Maithanai says empathetically. "Are you feeling nervous at all?"

Diwa takes a long, hard look at her cousin, but doesn't respond. Maithanai wasn't that much older than Diwa. Yet she was still unmarried, a fact that Diwa couldn't help be intensely jealous of.

She looks her up and down, and takes another sip of her tea.

Must be because of her hawk nose.

"a'Maitha, don't you want to be out there?" Diwa says throwing Maithanai a grin cheeky enough to match her father's. "You know, maybe you too could find an a'Dirauj, or some wealthy merchant?"

Maithanai squints at Diwa seeing the insult behind the veil of sweetness.

"You want me gone from the tent again," Maithanai states matter-of-factly. "And you are being most cruel to drive me from here. I see what you are doing, but it won't work. Firstly, ao'Shiva would cut me from top to tail. And secondly, then I wouldn't be able to keep you calm before the wedding."

"I am calm. At least now I am. I'll admit the idea of running did cross my mind before," Diwa flicks her eyes to the entrance, to the music and ceremony, "but after my meeting with akal'Jhealo-... I think- I think I'm excited for this. I'll be going to Shanomzeh."

Maithanai whistles a long note.

"Of that I am jealous," she says, "but it will be from your husband's wishes. Not quite your own. Not quite *free to roam*."

Diwa snorts.

"Don't quote that Kaogarea to me," Diwa says.

"You know as well as I do that me and you aren't free to roam. We can't just travel away from here like Jheal will be able to. Or even Sha. No. Nobody here is truly *free to roam*. akal'Jhealo told me that only the Terkizcho Diraujzeh can grant true freedom. *Only* he has the power to do that. And he hasn't granted that to any of us."

Diwa looks to the floor and controls her breathing. She could feel she was getting too angry.

"But," she continues, "I'll be the one telling akal'Tijjikauz where we are going. That will be my freedom. Of that I'm sure."

Maithanai wrinkles her nose at the suggestion.

"I don't know about that... It seems to me that-".

A shout cuts through Maithanai's comment.

Both girls perk up.

"Was that part of the ceremony?" Maithanai asks.

Diwa shakes her head.

"I don't think so," she says looking at Maithanai wide-eyed.

"Then what in the shadel's name is going on out there," says Maithanai, urgency coursing through her voice.

They meet each other's eyes and jump to their feet, dashing towards the entrance.

Maithanai reaches the entrance first to look out.

"Don't look-" she says.

She holds out a hand to block Diwa, but it's a feeble attempt. Diwa pushes past to look.

The first thing she spots is the Terkizcho guardsmen's swords out and levelled at the tribespeople. They have boxed them in.

Diwa puts her hand over her mouth to stop herself making any noise.

The two girls watch in fright as a bloodied and cut up Terkizcho warrior push a bound outrider to the ground. The outrider has a rope wrapped roughly around his neck.

Realisation hits Diwa. She had seen that scout before. He was one of the men who she had seen report to her father when they got back to the Oasis. Diwa had only caught a glimpse of him while she was caring for Jalila and a'Sha but the scar across his mouth was unmistakeable. It was Shala.

The Hourglass That Swallows You

The bloodied Terkizcho moves back towards Tijjikauz and nods.

Tijjikauz's voice rings out.

"Kirajauz here," he says nodding towards the bloodied Terkizcho, "informs me that you have tried to raid my city. Why I ask? Aren't we supposed to be allies? And to make matters worse you have killed my friend, Shiv'Anu."

He lets the words settle before continuing.

"He says *this man* here aided that attack..."

He all but spits at Shala.

"By your laws and ours you have broken the gold oath you have made."

Tijjikauz looks to the ground before quickly coming to a decision.

"You all will face consequences for this betrayal-... this treachery. But *he* must die. Now."

The Dirauj looks around for any dissenting opinion, and is met only by the hard faces of the desert 'Ifacho. A few of the tribespeople put their hands on their weapons. The scout shakes his head at them.

Tijjikauz takes a step in front of Shala, and drags him up by the hair.

"What do you have to say for yourself," says Tijjikauz.

"We. Did. Nothing-" says Shala through pained breaths.

"Is that all you have to say? You must take me for a fool."

Tijjikauz throws him down forcefully.

He signals to one of his guards, a man holding one arm as if it or his shoulder were hurt.

"Kill the traitor," Tijjikauz says.

Shala turns to look Tijjikauz in the eye.

The guard nods, then takes a dagger with his good hand and stabs the scout in the back.

Shala grunts as the dagger pierces deep into his back, but keeps his gaze on Tijjikauz. As the blood fills his mouth he spits defiantly at the Dirauj's feet.

The guardsman drags the dagger out of Shala's back.

He falls on his face, light dragged out of his eyes.

Diwa lets out a gasp as the scout falls to the ground.

"Anyone here object to this killing," Tijjikauz says to the crowd with his arms wide.

He was inviting dissent.

To Diwa his armour pulsed blood-red as the waves of firelight hit it.

"No? Good. We shall-".

A woman's yell erupts from the crowd. Diwa recognised it as Shala's betrothed.

"For Shala!"

A dagger flies from the gathered 'Ifacho towards Shala's murderer. It hits him hard, embedding into his good shoulder, before he can turn back towards the crowd.

The 'Ifacho let loose a wild war yell.

The green-flash illuminates the sky before Diwa is dragged back into the tent by Maithanai. The green shawl covers the desert and lights up her tent.

Within moments a woman's body crashes through the entrance of the tent impaled by a sword through her chest.

Diwa screams.

SHA

THE BRILLIANT GREEN light is fierce but short-lived. As it is a byproduct of the two worlds being so close to each other it lasts mere moments.

Sha can't put into thought everything he is experiencing.

His senses are stinging.

His eyes were glazed.

He was in a state of pure reaction.

Around him the green light was already beginning to fade.

His mother, over in the distance, turns away and walks out over the sand.

And he knew that if he didn't get to her now, he will never see her again.

With a great effort he escapes his Uncle's grasp and tries to run towards his mother.

He is shouting her name, shouting for her to come back, for her not to leave him alone here.

He feels like he is running forever, but in a few short steps he is swept up into his Uncle's arms again.

Sha's throat hurts, both inside and out. His voice isn't loud, despite his best efforts, and it is faltering.

His neck feels like fire.

He bites at his Uncle, scratches at him like some wild fox.

All the while shouting out for his mother to come back to him, to take him away from his Uncle. For all of this to not be happening.

He can't see it through his grief and incomprehension, but around him his Uncle is crying.

The iron grip of his Uncle is too strong to break out of.

Then like hearing the silence of the shore he starts to hear the waves of the present.

His Uncle's voice filters through the aether.

"I'll teach him to think a'Jali. I will. I promise you that."

Slowly but surely Sha begins to calm as the figure of his mother reaches further and further into the horizon.

Until it is just him and his uncle, sitting on the sand.

Sha doesn't know when or how they both got seated but his Uncle is still hugging him tight.

He can't tell when his mother disappeared, was it just a moment ago or hours ago.

He looks up to the night sky.

Godshome and the moon are still hanging up there. The flash wasn't too long ago and another threatens to fill the sky.

Behind him a ruckus is happening.

He hears the distant sound of steel on steel. When did it turn from music to agony?

Heavy footsteps approach from behind. Sha recognises the sound as feet and armour rushing towards them and turns.

He recognises the big man, Shi'Auz as he approaches. He is holding his side. He looks hurt.

"Fu'Aitauz. The Dirauj has started a war. We need you."

"What's happening?" Asks Mald shooting to his feet.

Before Shi'Auz can respond Mald pushes him to the floor.

Mald then ducks also, but as quick as he is he can't quite escape the sword cutting the top of his hairline as the Terkizcho horseman rushes past.

Blood runs down his face.

The horseman turns his horse for another run at them.

Mald was ready.

The horseman leans down as he rides towards them to swipe again at Mald.

At the last second Mald moves like some sort of desert snake towards the horseman, dodging his blade. With a strength belying his size he grabs his leg and pulls.

The horseman topples off of the horse with a heavy thud, losing his sword in the process. Before the horseman can get up Shi'Auz whacks him with skull-shattering thud across his head.

"Terkizcho horsemen," he spits on the ground. "Not worthy of their horses."

Mald and Shi'Auz then both turn back to the wedding. They run off at speed.

"Stay here," Mald orders Sha over his shoulder.

Sha doesn't move. He still isn't thinking clearly. He turns to look back over to the overhang. He walks over to it to try and find his mother.

Getting to it he climbs on top, and stares out over the desert.

The ocean of sand lay bare before him. The moonlit dunes merge and swirl into the pin-pricked fabric of the midnight sky, while the brilliant blue and green pearl of 'Ifa Shadelna overwhelms the moon.

Yet he can't find his mother no matter how hard he squints.

Deflated, he loses the will to stand, so he sits in the sand.

He rubs his eyes with his hands.

Absent-mindedly he glances around and spots the yellow box left abandoned beside him.

He stretches over to inspect it.

Picking it up it feels surprisingly light.

His hands find the latches on either side. With a firm press they both spring open with a loud pop and the box opens up gently.

Inside is a short L-shaped metal object unlike any he had ever seen, surrounded by a thick yet airy fabric. He pushes the fabric and finds it bounces back against his fingers easily.

His head unconsciously bends towards his shoulder as he inspects the contents.

Surrounded by the perfectly cut fabric were three bronze-coloured cylinders that glinted dully in the upper right corner of the box. Tenderly he picks up the cylinders one by one to inspect them each in turn. They each look exactly the same. A light bronze colouring for what must have been the body, with a dark leaden colour forming to a rounded tip.

Without really thinking he puts the dull bronze cylinders into his pockets.

Then he sets his sights on the L-shaped object made of metal. It was heavy, made up of a large tube, followed by a fatter, shorter, honey-combed cylinder in the back. Underneath, it had a rough handle made of a material he couldn't place. It could have been wood, but he didn't think it was. It felt more like the yellow box that it came in.

It was unlike anything he had ever seen.

He wraps his hand around the handle. It was clearly too big for him but it felt... designed. What was even more curious however was that, despite the size, his index finger naturally sat on a small metal lever near the base of the corner of the L.

There was another metal lever on top.

He couldn't resist pulling it back.

It clicked.

Off in the distance he hears a war-yell, the dull clanking of armoured feet on sand.

Something in him screamed at him to turn.

He jumps up and spins around to face the distant warrior.

He was less than five paces from him.

It wasn't Mald or the big man. It was someone he didn't know. A Terkizcho with his sword raised was running at full speed towards him.

All Sha can do is open his mouth as his body stiffens in fear.

Thunder explodes from his hands, from the metal rod, along with a cloud of smoke.

It leaves his ears as fast as it came, leaving in its wake an all encompassing ringing that deafens his ears to everything.

He sees the swordsman fall towards him with speed carried on by his momentum.

He crashes on top of Sha with the weight of a dead body.

Sha can feel himself scream, but can't hear it. He frantically tries to push the body off of him but isn't strong enough.

He can't hear.

He can't move.

He can't breathe.

He can't even scream.

All he can do is scratch and claw, but his fingers were beginning to tingle as his arms went numb.

With each second that passes he can feel his vision getting darker and darker.

And he is losing.

Like a starburst in the deep dark, light floods his darkened vision.

He feels his lungs expand outwards and gulps down air as it becomes available to him.

He sees big arms grab the underside of the Terkizcho and haul the body aside.

Sha drags himself away, and spins around to crawl.

He feels a muscled grip hoist him to his feet.

Unsteady on his feet he bends over forward to take in gulps of air.

Looking up he sees Shi'Auz mouthing something he can't hear. The ringing still pulsing through his ears.

The big man grabs his hand and wrenches Sha towards him.

Sha stumbles as the big man drags him with speed towards a small dune on the outskirts of the camp.

Quickly they reach the top and the big man signals for Sha to duck down with him. Sha complies quickly and hunches down beside him. Almost as a glance Sha looks out over the dune.

From their small vantage point they can see most of the camp. A fire has started among the tents near the outer edge casting an amber glow across the dark shadows. Within the oasis, however, the fighting has stopped. Only just.

In the corners and where they can hide Sha can see 'Ifacho women and children cowering in fear incase the battle begins anew.

In the centre stand Mald and Ilatr, with their weapons drawn and looking defiant. Like lions.

It was all happening too fast. Sha was having difficulty processing the situation. From the darkness of his vision to the overwhelming ringing pulsing in his ears.

Opposite them Sha recognised the warrior of legend that his Uncle had fought with, raided with, in his golden armour. Beside Tijjikauz was another guardsman Sha didn't recognise. But he looked vicious even from this distance.

Mald and Ilatr on one side, and Tijjikauz and his guardsman exchange loud and angry words but Sha can't make out anything they are saying past the emotion. Let alone through the ringing in his head.

Tijjikauz points to his guardsman, covered in blood, and Sha can just make out a name, "Kirajauz."

This provokes something between the sides and tensions suddenly flare.

Ilatr begins shouting.

Tijjikauz is red in the face with rage.

Kirajauz looks like he could spit venom.

Mald looks ice cold by comparison.

Sha stares at his uncle.

This look meant thoughtfulness and restraint, but Sha knew to look further. Deeper. It meant anger was being honed to a fine point.

And it scared him.

Mald speaks softly.

Kirajauz launches himself at him, but is easily swept aside by Ilatr.

The Terkizcho hits the sand on his back hard. He curls on the ground, spluttering.

Ilatr then kicks the downed Kirajauz towards the Dirauj.

Tensions flare again.

Ilatr stares at the Dirauj with a fire in his eyes that Sha had never seen before.

Like a viper, Kirajauz gets to his feet. Despite being shaky on his feet he is completely focused. The Terkizcho tenses as he grabs a sheathed short sword from his belt, but with a short sharp command is stopped by Tijjikauz.

Then he spits at Ilatr's feet and in a smooth motion moves into the shadows a few steps away to grab something.

He comes out dragging Jheal by the scruff of his neck.

Kirajauz puts his sword to his throat.

Mald's eyes catch the fire light and his nostrils flare with unfiltered hatred and disgust. Sha had never seen him like *this* before. The ice was broken, melted.

Mald points at Tijjikauz and shouts.

Despite the ringing Sha could almost feel the words.

Move the blade, or die.

Mald levels his sword at Tijjikauz with a smooth upwards motion, pointing directly between his eyes.

Ilatr puts his hand out and onto the top of the flat edge of Mald's sword to lower it.

Mald doesn't.

He leaves it levelled, and stares down the edge of his sword and towards the Dirauj.

Ilatr says something to him Sha can't make out.

Mald shakes his head at him, but doesn't take his eye off of the Dirauj.

Then Ilatr points around him. Sha follows the motion and sees carnage. The fires are getting bigger. 'Ifacho men, women and children are slowly bleeding out, while others are cowering in fear.

On the other side Terkizcho guardsmen are crawling towards their brothers-in-arms, to get away from the fires as much as to get medical aid, who are doing their best to help.

Mald finally takes his eyes off of the Dirauj and looks around.

As he takes it all in his sword begins to lower.

Ilatr nods and then walks towards Tijjikauz with his head high.

Kirajauz tightens the sword against the boy's throat.

Ilatr stops and puts his arms above his head. Then, awkwardly, he bows before the Dirauj with his forehead to the ground.

Kirajauz takes his sword away from the boy's throat, but still holds him close. He looks to Tijjikauz for a command.

It's given with a nod.

Released Jheal runs over to Mald and hugs him as hard as he can.

Mald drops his sword as he embraces his only son. Yet he doesn't take his eyes off of Tijjkauz.

Despite the blur, despite the lack of understanding of the situation, something in that stare shocks Sha down to the core. It was a look he had never known of his Uncle. A look into those eyes was like a glimpse into the depths of hatred.

Mald whispers something into his son's ear.

Jheal frantically shakes his head and hugs his father harder.

Another nod from Tijjikauz.

Within a few steps Kirajauz is in front of Mald and Jheal. With brute force he yanks the boy out of his father's grasp.

Mald holds out his hand but doesn't move.

Sha can only just lip read the words from his mouth.

I'll come for you, he says.

The world seems to hang on a knife's edge.

With the boy back on his side Tijjikauz signals for his men to leave.

Mald stands. All he can do is look on.

A scuffle from the large wedding tent steals Sha's attention. He turns his head to see a dark-skinned Terkizcho come out with Diwa in one hand and Maithanai in the other. The grasp seems light but must be like iron. No amount of pulling or struggling from the girls can free them.

With a rough shove he pushes Diwa up into a saddle and then forces Maithanai behind her.

Talia runs, wild eyed, out of a nearby tent towards her two eldest children.

Before she knows it Mald catches her and holds her close. She struggles, scratches, shouts as she tries to get to her children yet Mald holds her close and firm.

Shiva appears by her side and hugs them both, as much to hold Talia back as herself.

Jheal tries to break out of Kirajauz's arms but is met by excessive force. The Terkizcho punches Jheal hard in the stomach. The boy's face explodes as the wind is knocked out of him.

Mald loses it.

He breaks out of Shiva and Talia's grasp leaving the women to fall to the ground. But before he can get more than a few paces he is met by three of his own 'Ifacho, who hold him back.

Ilatr stands and walks in front of his Fu'Aitauz. He bows his head forward slightly.

Mald slows his struggle against his men and breathes deeply. Then with an effort he puts his forehead to Ilatr's.

Ilatr pulls back and turns towards the Dirauj. Beside him Kirajauz has the unconscious Jheal over his shoulder.

The fire is beginning to alarm the 'Ifacho. The flames are getting larger and larger, more and more out of control.

The Dirauj gives the final signal for his people to move.

They turn and walk in formation, leaving the dead behind.

. . .

The moon is near to the earth as Tijjikauz and his men ride over the first dune back towards Kiraj'it'Jalila. Trailing behind them are a scattering of the tribesmen and women, bound and dragged, being lead towards imprisonment.

Sha has been unable to move from the ridge all this time. His mind is blank, broken. He sees without seeing, and can only hear that overwhelming ringing.

In the camp the 'Ifacho are trying their hardest to get the fire under control.

The big man, Shi'Auz, holds the boy's hand as he protectively leads him down to the camp. With a gesture he tells Sha to stay still outside of the range of the fire.

Sha sits on the sand.

From the camp his grandmother and aunt come towards him and hug him close.

Then in turn they pull away and move to help fight the fire in any way they can.

From the fire he sees Mald. His eyes are red and bloodshot. His face is blackened by smoke.

The 'Ifacho fight a losing battle against the wildfire until first light.

Sha can only sit in the sand and watch.

MALD

His arms felt like lead, and swung heavy by his sides.

His legs felt like stone, each step he took threatened to make him collapse.

He felt broken. His movements weren't guided by his mind but rather his body was dragging his mind.

His mouth tasted of grit and ash.

With some effort he takes out his side flask and takes a sip.

It was empty.

In a flash of rage he throws it across the sand towards the cinders of his once-living oasis.

They had done their best to keep the livestock and people alive, but it was at the cost of his shelter.

The perpetual hourglass turned once again on his people.

His first instinct was to spot his family, and within an instant he felt a stabbing in his heart. a'Jhea and a'Di were nowhere to be seen.

The others, Shiva, Talia, even his little one were each attending to whatever chore they could still accomplish.

Of his people, some were trying to move water, some trying to rebuild.

Even a'Jali was gone.

How could he lose so much, so fast.

He wasn't fast enough. He wasn't ruthless enough. He wasn't strong enough.

Above him a maithane bird chirps, and flies off to the west. It must be flying to another one of his shelters.

This place was a shelter, but not their final home.

The thought strikes him. They weren't tied to this place. The maithane flitter between east and west with the wind.

They must move again like the maithane, to another shelter. They had many such secret places.

This place is done.

But his people aren't.

We will rebuild.

We will endure.

Mald puts his hands to his face to rub his bloodshot eyes, leaving an ashen mark.

Today will be tough.

Tomorrow will be even tougher.

But we are tougher still.

With some effort he gets himself to his feet and whistles loudly to gain everyone's attention.

He is met with scattered acknowledgement.

This is the best that they can manage right now, and that is fine.

"We have lost today. We have lost much. But we are still here. We-," he clutches at his heart as he is left breathlessness.

Darkness begins to vignette his vision.

He starts to fall- and feels hands catch him. Shiva and his wife lower him slowly to the ground.

He sits cross-legged on the sand, desperately trying to claw back his breath. Shiva offers him her water.

Talia's voice rings out.

"Our hearts are broken. My heart is broken. We have lost. Yet still we stand here. We have ever been the Dirauj's spear and shield in the sea of sand. We thought we ruled together. But he has done nothing but take, and grow fat on our bloodshed. He has taken my daughter. My son. Our family. Your family. Even this sanctuary from us."

Talia looks at Mald.

"But he isn't one of us. He never has been. I know now that he has never been. He views us as tools. Not equals."

The gathered 'Ifacho begin to dissent.

"Never!" Comes a call from the crowd.

"No!" Comes another call.

"We must take the fight to him."

"We must burn Kiraj. Burn the dirauj!" Comes another call with a resounding cry of approval.

"Wait-," Talia is losing control of the crowd. They are tired, but there is rage in their hearts.

A sharp long whistle comes from beside her as Mald gets to his feet again.

"Ilatr is gone. a'Diwa is gone. a'Jheal is gone. a'Jali is gone," his arms sway with the weight of leaden fists. "This place is gone. Our fists clutch at sand while it falls away faster than ever. But we are here. The Dirauj has taken too much. The Dirauj is too strong. We need strength to fight back, yet right now we do not have it."

Mald holds his fist to the shadow of 'Ifa Shadelna, and releases it, allowing the other planet to rest in his palm.

"By the shadel and my family I swear, before I take the final walk he will pay. He thinks of us as tools. He thinks we will bend to him if he takes our hearts and threatens them. He has forgotten his own past, and who we are. For now we will be his tools, fight this war. Until we have the means to crush him. He thinks he has broken us. That we will be his dogs. Well... this dog will bite him when he stumbles. That is my position. We do not forget. And we will not forgive. When I take the walk, I will drag him behind me in chains."

His tribe around him remain silent.

A few grumble and balk at the idea.

Alexander Albret

This will be a tough medicine to swallow. Playing as his tools will be too much for some.

Mald sits back down and puts his head in his hands.

The tribe will splinter, but he will protect what he can.

Even if he has to sacrifice his heart and mind to do it, he will get back his family.

He will have his vengeance.

JALILA - EPILOGUE

In the desert, somewhere between the moon falling and the sun rising Jalila wanders between life and death.

She looks up towards where Godshome rests suspended in the night sky.

As she stares at the other world she sees what looks like a candle blossom on the dark side of the planet and quickly flick out.

a'Sha will never believe what she just saw. I'll have to remember to tell him about it.

While staring up at the other world, she stumbles.

The world spins as she falls. She hits the sand hard and begins to roll.

Painful moments later she finds herself lying face down.

Someway down this dune the sand had been melted into glass.

She rolls over…

And sees what halted her fall.

The Terkizcho body smelt fresh. Dead but only very recently, not long enough for it to go rancid.

She puts her hands onto the body to try and lift herself up. Her hands find out what killed the Terkizcho as they fall through a large gaping hole in the back of the soldier.

Not finding anything solid on the body she falls on top of him.

She doesn't have the strength to try to push herself up again.

Just some rest. That's all I need. Let's just stay here for a moment.

Unable to move her head much she peers around as best she can.

Her good eye looks up and sees a hole in the side of a melted silver star.

Oh. Where did that come from?

Around her was smouldering black glass. And in the centre of it all was this star. It must have fallen from a very large height to create a crater as big as this.

A glow from the hole in the centre of the star grabs her attention.

She sees, sitting within it, a very large man skewered by a Terkizcho spear.

He was larger than any she had seen before. Even the northmen guards of the Fergilna Court were small in comparison.

Around the skewered man pretty red and green lights sparkle and fade.

a'Sha would love those lights. I'll show them to him when I get back...

Her head falls softly onto the Terkizcho as she loses the strength to keep it up.

...And a'Ma will want to see this too... I'll have to remember where this is.

First, I think I just need to close my eyes for a moment.

Just a little nap to regain my strength.

Only for a little while.

There, face down, ao'Jalila, sister of akal'Mald, daughter of ao'Shiva and akal'Kali, never feels anything ever again.

Appendix I.

The 'Ifacho Kaogarea' (lit. "Want of the Homeless")

--- 1 ---

1. I ask again, where is my home?
2. Where once stood the monuments and walls
3. now lie a single stone.
4. A stone etched with our love
5. and scared by our parting.
6. When I turned to the desert endless,
7. so long ago, in hope and cause,
8. my tears and heart broke over that single stone.
9. Free to choose where we roam,
10. But ever to roam alone.

--- 2 ---

1. Now here I see where you roamed,
2. old tents and the memory of them.

3. How you must have draped yourself in mourning clothes.
4. I see where your tears, mixed with blood, fell.
5. More than once I turned back towards the stone,
6. More than once I wept as the warm winds threatened the storm,
7. More than once the memory came back with the yearly rain.
8. How did we deny such love?
9. When here I can see the etching and the scarring,
10. the fountain of shadow birthed from that stone.

--- 3 ---

1. Once again the endless desert brings the warm winds.
2. Once again I have turned back towards the stone.
3. Once again I look for where you roam.
4. Now here, too late- it wasn't so far as it felt.
5. But the endless desert made it far.

--- 4 ---

1. Now, the Sun and it's Dark Twin awake to chase each other,
2. slowly, inevitably, their glory unending.
3. Below a fox catches a scorpion,
4. and in turn is caught by an eagle-owl.
5. In it's flight I hear the crack,
6. and another shadow must roam to find the Dark Twin.
7. Another shadow to join the silent cacophony.
8. I feel and see the eternal turning flame, that heavy hourglass.
9. Where you roam, I too will roam,
10. and where I roam, you too will roam again.

The Hourglass That Swallows You

--- 5 ---

1. Here I am an eternal fugitive in a land without chains,
2. and behind and in front are all my shadows.
3. Verily, I shall forever tread on all my shadows.
4. I must roam the endless desert, the land shadows gather,
5. Forever my home.

--- 6 ---

1. And in the endless desert I see again the single stone.
2. It's etching and scars fading in the sun and wind,
3. but those children of the shadows remain.
4. My heart weeps as the children of shadow remind me of you,
5. and my shadow will continue to roam to find you.
6. But those shadows who keep my company have grown
7. and in turn have cast their shadow on all the endless desert.
8. Their shadow will keep me roaming.
9. Their shadow protects me from the eternal turning flame.
10. Will the shadow last eternal? I ask again, where is my home?

Appendix II.

Glossary of Terms

'SHADEL ['.SHA.DEL] : SPIRIT, SOUL - LIT. "'SHA" fox, "del" eye, or fox eye

a'Jali : a' + name usually denotes familiarity and affection between two people - lit. "A'" little, lesser, or small

akal'Mald : akal' + name denotes respect, gendered male

'Ifa Shadelna ['.i.fa sha.del.na] : Godshome, a name for the wandering planet - lit. "'Ifa" Home, "Shadel" Spirit, "-na" equivalent to English 's

Ul-Fergilna [ul fer.gil.na] : Language of the Fergil - lit. "Ul" Word, "Fergil" People from Fergil, "-na" equivalent to English 's

Fergil [fer.gil] : The name of the Western Eye Empire, People from the River Fergil

ao'Shiva : ao' + name denotes respect, gendered female

'Ifacho ['.i.fa.cho] : Our Tribespeople's name – lit. "'Ifa" home, "cho" negative, or homeless

Kiraj'it'Jalila [ki.rai.it.ja.li.la] : Tower by the Sea, or city on the shore – lit. "Kiraj" tower/fortress, "'it'" next to, "Jalila" sea/shore

Parfi'at [par.fi.'.at] : First Stable, or Old Horse Stables – lit. "Par" first/old/before, "Fi'at" stables

Dirauj [di.rauw] : Shah, King – lit. "dirauj" crowned man

Fergilna [fer.gil.na] : 'Ifacho affiliated with the Fergil – lit. "fergil" People of the Fergil, "na" equivalent to the English 's, or owned by

Terkizcho [ter.kiz.cho] : The name for the Eastern Eye Empire's people – lit. "Terkiz" to speak, "cho" negative, or mute

a'ijd [ah.'.ea.d] : lit. Mother

Fu'Aitauz [fu.'.ait.auws] : Cavalry Leader, or Leader – lit. "fu'ait" horse, "-auz" equivalent to English -er, eg. Carpenter

Kaogarea' [kao.ga.Rea.'] : used to refer to the 'Ifacho Kaogarea' or 'Ifacho Poem - lit. "kaogarea'" to want or desire

Maithane [mai.tha.ne] : Red-Crested Oasis Bird – lit. "Maith" Bird, "Ane" red

ao'Dirauj [ow.di.row.] - Queen without the connotation of being subservient to a king - lit. "Ao'" Female, "Dirauj" king

Aiwash [I.wa.sh] – Camel Stables – lit. "aiwash" camel stables

Diraujcho [di.row.cho] - False king, or usurper - lit. "Dirauj" King, "cho" negative, or Not King

Faijh a'ilatr [fai.jh.a.il.at.r]: side small sword, or dagger held on the side - lit."Faijh" side, "a'" lesser, "ilatr" sword

Shanomzeh [sha.nom.zeh] : Ul-Terkizcho (from the language of the Terkizcho) lit. Settlement Big, or City

Diraujzeh [di.rauw.zeh] : Greater King – lit. "Dirauj" king, "zeh" Terkizcho word meaning greater.

About the Author

Alexander Albret is a debut fantasy author whose passion for world-building and storytelling has culminated in this first book of the *Timeshome* series, *The Hourglass That Swallows You*.

He is a passionate reader and explorer of myth and legend, and draws inspiration from those ancient myths, diverse cultures, and the natural world to craft vivid, immersive worlds.

When not writing, Alex (also known as Sol) is a filmmaker and musician, with three full-length albums with the band *Brain Ape*.

He lives in London, UK with his wife, cat and dog.

X x.com/TimeshomeMedia
instagram.com/timeshomemedia

Milton Keynes UK
Ingram Content Group UK Ltd.
UKHW020958261124
451531UK00024B/96